Punch

with Judy

Punch
with Judy

Avi

Illustrated by Emily Lisker

AN AVON  CAMELOT BOOK

AVON BOOKS
A division of
The Hearst Corporation
1350 Avenue of the Americas
New York, New York 10019

Copyright © 1993 by Avi Wortis
Interior illustrations copyright © 1993 by Emily Lisker
Published by arrangement with Bradbury Press
Visit our website at **http://AvonBooks.com**
Library of Congress Catalog Card Number: 92-27157
ISBN: 0-380-72980-6
RL: 5.9

First Avon Camelot Printing: September 1997
First Avon Flare Printing: October 1994

CAMELOT TRADEMARK REG. U.S. PAT. OFF. AND IN OTHER COUNTRIES, MARCA REGISTRADA, HECHO EN U.S.A.

Printed in the U.S.A.

OPM 10 9 8 7 6 5 4 3 2 1

For Natalie Babbitt

PART
ONE

PART
ONE

One

One raw day in 1870—five years after the Civil War—a man came upon a boy. The man's face was round and ruddy, with blue eyes which fairly sparked laughs upon the world. The boy was pale and scrawny, with eyes barely able to steal glances. The man wore new boots. They boy's bare feet were caked with mud. The man's purple coat was warm. The boy shivered in rags. And it was a rakish top hat which sat on the man's head, whereas the boy had placed his hat—an old cloth one—on the muddy ground before him. For he was begging pennies by performing a shuffle of timid twists, jittery jumps, and sudden stops. The cap, however, was empty.

Looking on, the man suppressed a laugh; he'd seen puppets show more life than this boy. At the same time, he felt inclined to hoot at a performance he considered an insult to the arts *he* served.

The boy did have another audience: three loafers with slack faces who watched, chewed tobacco, and spat. It was only when the boy attempted a grand finale—a kicking up of his heels which served to lay him out, facedown in the mud—that the three laughed so long and loud they had to hug themselves to keep together.

And when they realized the boy was not going to dance anymore, they went off—though still they laughed.

As for the purple-coated man, he shrugged and began to go too, only to stop and—thinking about the way those loafers laughed—glance back. The boy was sitting in the mud, pawing his eyes like a half-drowned cat.

What, the man asked himself, had the boy done to make those loafers laugh so?

Feeling a mix of contempt and pity, the man started off, only to pause and study the boy yet again. Then, casually, he strolled back and dropped a coin into the boy's cap. The boy, taken by surprise, looked up.

"Sure, it's yours," the man said, with an accent which marked him as raised in Ireland. "You worked hard enough for it." He judged the boy to be no more than eight years of age.

The boy snapped the coin up with a dirty hand, then scrambled to his feet and stood with a bowed head.

"Is this the place you call your home?" the man

demanded, gesturing to the snarl of shacks and shanties that stood beyond.

The boy, who wasn't sure where he came from, said nothing.

"Where do you hail from, then?"

The boy had no more notion regarding *that* question than he did the first, so again he gave no response.

"Well then," the man persisted, "what about the folks who feed you the odd bit of bread?"

The boy only shrugged.

Increasingly bemused, the man went on. "Well, surely now," he asked, "you own a name, don't you?"

Since, other than "Hey, you!" or "You, fool!" the boy had no name, he remained mute.

At this the man grew thoughtful. Then he said, "Perform that thing-a-ding again. The same as you done before."

"The what?" the boy replied at last.

"Your bit of a turvy jig. The turn that made those men go double daft with laughter."

When the boy did not move, the man jangled some

coins within his pocket. "Yours," he coaxed, "if you dance."

The boy knew there was only one way to get the coins. So, though exhausted, he danced like he'd done before, but soon ran down like a windup toy with a broken spring.

The man grinned and offered up his coin. The boy— though he dared not check the value—grabbed it with such clumsy haste that the man laughed out loud.

"And you're absolutely sure you have neither kith nor kin?" he wanted to know.

Ashamed to acknowledge the truth of it all, the boy gazed at his toes.

"All right then," the man said, "you might as well come with me.

Now the boy looked up, his face a mix of hope and fear.

"I've got a traveling medicine show," the man explained. " 'Joe McSneed and His Merry Men,' it's called. I'm Mr. McSneed himself, the grand boss of it all. If you want yourself a place, it's yours."

"A place?"

"You can be my insurance policy."

The boy had no idea what *that* meant.

"Mind," Mr. McSneed said, "if you don't want the job, you needn't bother yourself a moment to excess." So saying, he wheeled about on his fine heeled boots and marched off like a proud rooster.

The boy, uncertain if he should believe the man or not, watched him go. Then he looked at the new coin. It was a whole dollar, more money than he'd ever beheld before.

Now the truth is, the boy had no place to live. Nor had he eaten for two entire days. No doubt that was why, limping, as was his way, he began to follow after Mr. Joe McSneed.

TWO

Mr. McSneed led the boy to where his troupe was quartered, the common in the middle of town. There, on a field of sparse grass, three bright wagons formed a backdrop to a wooden performing ring. Stands had been erected around the other half, while not far off a trio of sleek horses grazed. The largest wagon—placed between the smaller ones—was roofed, with windows and a door at the rear. On either side was a sign which read:

JOE McSNEED & HIS MERRY MEN
UNDER THE DIRECT PATRONAGE OF
MRS. McSNEED!
CONTORTIONIST SUPREME
WHO IS ACTUALLY
THE BANISHED QUEEN OF TIPPERARY!
WITH BELLE THE WONDER HORSE
& MR. TWIGLET!
JUGGLER EXTRAORDINARY!

7

ALSO, VERY SPECIAL !
Dr. PUDLOW'S
NE-NIP—The Medicine of the Ancients
It Will Cure Whatever Ails You!!!
AND BLODGER, the AFRICAN ACROBAT!
ALSO COUNT ZUNBADDEN,
RUSSIAN ANIMAL TRAINER
AND INTRODUCING JUDY !
ELEGANT EQUESTRIAN

The boy—who cold not read—still was dazzled by it.

Seated on this wagon's backboard was Mrs. Molly McSneed. She was a small, lithe woman, buxom as a proud hen, with jade-green eyes set like jewels in a pale face framed by brick-red hair. She was reading a newspaper.

"My darling wife," Mr. McSneed announced as he approached, "I return like the bee to the red rose."

The little lady set her paper aside. "Did you bring me a present, Mr. McSneed?" she asked, all dimples and smiles.

"I did, my dear, I did," Mr. McSneed returned, laughing the laugh of a man who's heard a joke he's eager to share. When Mr. McSneed laughed, Mrs. McSneed laughed. That was their way. Always.

"What have you brought me this time?"

"My love," Mr. McSneed said, beckoning to the boy, "may I introduce you to the newest member of our troupe."

8

The boy, clutching the dollar coin deep within his pocket, slumped forward.

Mrs. McSneed looked at the boy, at her husband, at the boy a second time, then again at her husband. "Mr. McSneed," she said severely, the laughter having drained from her face, "is this some sort of a joke?"

"My dear," her husband replied, "I've never been more serious in all my life."

After studying the boy for the third time, Mrs. McSneed drew her coat collar tightly about her neck. "Mr. McSneed," said she, "we don't need another child. We've got Judy, as sweet a daughter as ever was. May I be so bold as to ask what you'll *do* with this . . . person?"

"Now, love," Mr. McSneed returned, "you know yourself how well the show is booming. And it's all because of you, a true Banished Queen of Tipperary if ever there was one. But what we're lacking—it's the way of all first-class shows—is an *insurance* policy. That's what the lad shall be: insurance."

Mrs. McSneed examined the boy anew. He was staring at the ground, one foot rubbing another foot while a dirty hand wiped a gummy nose.

"Insurance," Mrs. McSneed said archly. "Isn't that farfetched? And your Merry Men won't like the hint."

Mr. McSneed drew himself up. "I'm sole boss of this troupe," he snapped. "I don't consult a soul."

"Not even—I gather—me."

"Pulse of my heart, you're as fine a performer as ever tripped on board or brick, but I've yet to meet the gal who can run a show. Still, you're perfectly right to urge proper introductions."

Mrs. McSneed, her face as pale as vanilla ice and

just as cold, returned, "And Judy, husband o' mine? Will you be insulting her as you've just done me?"

"I'll tell Judy what I intend to tell the Merry Men: The boy's to be company servant."

"As you wish. Does the boy come with a name?"

"I've decided," replied Mr. McSneed with a renewed smile, "to call him—*Punch.*"

Mrs. McSneed eyed her husband narrowly. "Punch *and* Judy, Mr. McSneed?"

"Exactly."

"As in the foolish flummery that features a desperate Judy and her devilish husband, Punch, enacting a tragic tale of love gone poor?"

"Rather," Mr. McSneed returned with a waggish wink, "that old drama of true love that never fails to provoke a laugh."

"Seems more like a Punch-*against*-Judy show you're concocting, my dear," drawled Mrs. McSneed, and she returned to her reading.

Mr. McSneed next led Punch to the four Merry Men, who were gathered around a dinner fire.

Mr. Twiglet, the senior member of the troupe, was in his seventies. Twig, as he was called, had a long neck, a chinless, mostly toothless mouth, a beakish nose and a balding head, on which perched a tattered brown derby. He was dressed in the multipocketed plaid coat he always wore, a coat which fit no better than a loose shell.

Next came Dr. F. X. Pudlow, company medicine-maker and illusionist. Doc had a belly which rounded pumpkinlike over his belt, as well as bandy little legs and a long white beard like Saint Nicholas himself.

Regarding Mr. Blodger, acrobat and keeper of equipment, he was a small, squinty-eyed black man, who, despite his size, was known for being fit as well as fierce. Blodger was forever twisting and folding his long, narrow fingers into knots, then cracking knuckles to make a sound like popcorn popping.

Finally, there was Mr. Zunbadden. He was a bald, bug-eyed, barrel-chested, pigeon-toed fellow, with a lantern jaw set below a mustache shaped like the horns of a bull. Zun talked little, smiled less, but did have a way with animals.

These were the four Merry Men.

"Gentlemen," Mr. McSneed announced as he thrust the reluctant boy forward, "may I introduce the newest member of our troupe. Goes by the name of Punch."

The four men studied Punch with hostile glares.

"What talent," Twig finally asked, "does this here Punch hide beneath his multiple layers of filth?"

"Company servants don't need talent," Mr. McSneed returned.

"As a medical man," Doc growled, "I'd opine he's not totally constituted for living."

"Nope," Zun added, "he don't look capable of bringing water to a dead mule."

"Of course," Blodget said with a pop of knuckles to make his point, "a dead mule might draw a crowd, while this boy, more than likely, will chase them away."

Mr. McSneed laughed, but said, "My dear Merry Men, he remains."

"You're boss on earth, Mr. McSneed," Twig said with a glance toward heaven.

Finally, Punch met Judy. Aged eleven, Judy had her mother's red hair with her da's blue eyes. Her freckled face, however, was very much her own. When Punch was brought to her, she was lying atop the black horse named Belle, gazing dreamily at the sky.

"Judy," Mr. McSneed called, "here's Mr. Punch."

Judy sat up. *"Punch?"* she cried. "Is that truly his name?"

"It is."

"Like the Punch of Punch and Judy?"

"Exact," her father said. "And newest member of our troupe."

Judy's nose wrinkled. "Da," she said, "I think you're teasing me."

"No, it's true."

"But Punch is supposed to be funny."

"Company servants don't need to be funny."

"Is that what he's to be for me?" Judy asked.

"I would suggest . . . a friend."

"Punch," Judy called. "Come here."

Alarmed, Punch looked to Mr. McSneed.

"You'll be wanting to do as she says," the man advised.

Punch inched forward.

"Da says we're to be friends," Judy said, and extended the back of her hand for Punch to kiss.

Punch stood there, bewildered.

Mr. McSneed laughed. Judy laughed, too, then touched heels to Belle's side and galloped off.

"Congratulations, Punch!" Mr. McSneed cried, giving the boy a clap to his shoulder that all but sent him sprawling. "You're a member of 'Joe McSneed and His Merry Men.'"

Punch, however, was staring after Judy. He was that smitten.

Three

During the next four years Punch traveled with Mr. McSneed and his troupe as they made their way through the eastern United States, performing acts and selling Ne-Nip. This Ne-Nip was a drink that Doc—who brewed it—claimed would cure most anything. Punch didn't know if this was true or not. Clearly it was sales of Ne-Nip which brought in the money that enabled "Joe McSneed and His Merry Men" to roam the countryside.

During those four years, Punch never performed in the show. Nor did he lose his limp, learn to stand very tall, nor manage to look anyone in the eye. Instead, he became exactly what Mr. McSneed said he'd become, company servant. That's to say, though Dr. Pudlow was the troupe's cook, Punch served the food. True, Mr. Blodger made and mended equipment, but it was Punch who set things right before, during, and after each performance. As for the animals, they were under Mr. Zunbadden's care, yet Punch was the one who fed and groomed them. And while Mrs. McSneed was in charge of costumes, it was barefoot Punch—no longer in rags, but in secondhand overalls—who cleaned the company boots.

During these four years, Mrs. McSneed never developed a liking for the boy. Not that she abused him; she just never took him to heart. Regarding Twig, Blodger, Doc, and Zun, they were more active in their dislike, flinging frowns—and now and again a kick—his way.

As for Judy, she was a performer and Punch the company servant. As promised, there was no word of "insurance policy" to her. But the two played together (Punch was the follower), talked together (Punch was the listener), ate together (Punch brought the food). And the truth was, Punch was happier with Judy than with anyone.

The boy's truest friend, however, was Mr. McSneed. If one of the Merry Men complained about Punch's uselessness, he would warn, "If he didn't do those tasks,

you would." If Mrs. McSneed suggested Punch was clumsy, he'd retort, "He'll prove deft enough." Or if Judy wondered why they bothered to keep Punch on, her father would snap, "Judy, love, be fair; will you be wanting to tramp with your parents for the whole of your life?"

This question always caused Judy to become dreamy-eyed. Then she'd admit, "I don't know yet."

"Well then, that's why he's here."

"That's not an answer!"

"Now, Judy, don't go legislating with questions. I'm boss here, and what I say goes for law."

"Yes, Da."

Now, when Punch joined "Joe McSneed and His Merry Men," times were good. Audiences were large. The company prospered. By doing what he was told, Punch earned his keep. And so it was for four fat years.

Then—it was in 1874—the whole nation sagged. Farmers couldn't sell their goods. Businesses failed. Workers had no jobs. Hardly a wonder that life grew hard for "Joe McSneed and His Merry Men" as well.

Then, to make matters truly bad, Mr. Joe McSneed himself, grand boss of the troupe, suffered a stroke and died.

PART
TWO

One

"I intend to bury Da proper," Judy was saying.

It was the seventh of August, two days after the death of Mr. McSneed. The troupe was camped in western Massachusetts, just beyond the town of New Moosup, their tattered tents pitched in a grove of skinny trees through which ran a muddy creek. Beyond lay nothing but poor farms and summer swallows chasing gnats.

Punch, who was listening to Twig and Judy argue, was seated on the ground, leaning against Alexander, a large black-and-white pig. The old man was juggling eggs. Juggling, he claimed, helped him think. As for Judy, she was perched on the backboard of the one wagon the troupe had managed to keep.

"What I'm saying, Judy," Twig replied, "is that it could be rough and risky if you go to Da's funeral."

"You're always expecting the worst," Judy threw back with fifteen-year-old sass.

"What about your ma?" Twig demanded.

"She'll stay here."

Punch scratched Alexander's back nervously. The pig grunted with contentment.

"Judy," Twig persisted, "it's my obligation to say

Da would disapprove. Remember his motto: Head Before Heart.''

"Don't speak for the dead," Judy retorted as she stamped into her boots.

"Why not?" Twig sputtered. "Saving the saints, they never hears."

"Maybe they do," Judy said.

The remark scandalized Twig so, one of his eggs hit his thumb and broke. The stench was awful, but rotten eggs looked fresh, and they were cheap, and cheapness was the fashion.

"Are you intending to bury the show as well as your da?" Twig demanded.

"Of course I'm not!" Judy exclaimed.

"Then why go?"

"Because I loved him!" Judy yelled with fury.

"Who didn't love Da?" Twig replied as the intact eggs vanished into his pockets. "Didn't I follow him for twenty years—from Ireland to America—to this forsaken place where he set off for the one place where Patrick Twiglet is not yet inclined to tour."

"He was trying to save the show!" Judy retorted.

"Wasn't I there when he married your ma!" Twig rushed on. "There, sweet girl, when you were born. There, when he hired each of the Merry Men! There, when our days were dipped in money thick as good beef gravy! There, when, with a momentary weakness of mind, he took in Punch here—when the lad is of no mortal use—then or now—to anyone!

" 'Joe McSneed and His Merry Men!' " Twig proclaimed, gesturing as if addressing a crowd. "From audiences of hundreds to a trickle of three! There were just *three* attending our last performance, Judy. Don't you forget it."

"Shhh!" Judy warned, glancing over her shoulder at the wagon behind. "Mama will hear you!"

"Little chance of that!" Twig exclaimed. "Since Da's death, your ma, the greatest contortionist in America, has been lying there"—he nodded to the wagon—"insensible! It'll take more than Doc's Ne-Nip to cure her."

Judy closed her eyes.

"Now, Judy," the juggler pressed, "Parson Cuthwhip is waiting at his church. And you know his boast, that though we're welcome to the funeral, he intends to have us horsewhipped out of town the moment Da goes down. I'm telling you, Judy, it's a good thing we pitched camp beyond the town line or, sure as breathing keeps man mortal, that town's sheriff—the ugly sod—would have broken our buttons by now. So all I'm saying is this: Let me and the boys do the honorable for Da. We can shift for ourselves. It's *you* that shouldn't be going."

"What about Punch?" Judy asked, for which the boy was grateful.

"Who cares bug's breath for Punch?" Twig sneered. "You're Da's kid, not him."

The remark turned Judy's cheeks ablaze.

"The thing is, Judy, it's you that's making the parson nervous—about his Horatio."

"Who?" Judy demanded.

"*Horatio.* His boy. You know right well the lad's been hanging around with eyes the size of moons for the sight of you."

"Oh, him," Judy said with a toss of fiery hair and a lift of nose.

"Punch," Twig said, "inform Judy about what that boy revealed."

Judy looked at Punch accusingly. "I don't care what Punch heard," she said.

"Do what your betters tell you, boy!" Twig cried, giving Punch a poke. "Tell Judy what that Horatio said!"

Going against Judy was the last thing Punch wanted. From the moment Da died, Judy had hardly said a word to him. Punch knew how much Judy had worshipped her da, so he assumed her silence was caused by grief. But he also sensed she was angry at *him.* That, he did *not* understand. Still, when Twig demanded he talk, he felt there was no choice.

With a sigh he said, "After our last performance, Horatio took me aside and told me his father was warning people against us. Called us thieves and sinners and told folks he'd have us treated so."

"You see, Judy," Twig exclaimed. *"that's* why we

had no audience. The parson is potentate hereabouts. Don't go tangling with his temptations."

Judy jumped up. "I'm going to the funeral."

"Judy," Punch suddenly cried, "what if the parson *does* get the sheriff to beat on us?"

Judy swung around to face him. "If you're too scared," she snapped, "stay. But I'm going." She began to walk off. Twig, looking baleful, followed.

Too upset to know what to do, Punch watched Judy and Twig march off. But Judy hadn't gone five steps before she whirled about and glared at Punch. "Da was like a father to you," she said with a scorn that scorched his heart. "The least you could do is honor his going."

Right then and there, Punch realized something: With Mr. McSneed—his protector—dead, he might be forced to leave the troupe. It was his worst nightmare. The thought so frightened him, he jumped up and hurried after Judy.

When Alexander the pig caught sight of Punch limping off, he scrambled after the boy. That was a comfort to Punch. Alexander may have been a pig—but at the moment he was the one friend Punch felt he could count on.

TWO

They set off for New Moosup, with Judy riding Belle, their one remaining horse. Punch, with Alexander at his side, held the bridle. Twig, Doc, Blodger, and Zun followed. Mrs. McSneed was left behind.

Hardly had the troupe gotten to the gates of the Old Conservative Just Established Original Church of New Moosup than Parson Cuthwhip dashed out.

He was a small man, this parson, wearing a suit of midnight black. Thin as a poker, with a blue-veined dart of a nose, he had eyes that were sharp as beads. "No animals allowed in these sacred precincts!" he cried, his fingers poking the air like pitchfork prongs. "None!"

Alarmed, Punch looked to Judy, but she only shrugged. Accordingly, Punch flung Belle's bridle over a post, then told Alexander to sit and stay. The pig did as he was told.

"Your father lies within," the parson intoned, beckoning Judy toward the church.

As they followed the parson, Punch saw—on either side of the walkway—three men. One was the sheriff of Coldspar County, Mr. Oxnard himself. Oxnard's stance suggested the prizefighter he once was, nose bent and lips flattened into a sneer. Small, gimlet eyes, partially

hidden behind scar tissue, were on the alert for sneak attacks. Punch thought him the meanest-looking man he'd ever seen.

A second man was large, black-bearded, and fierce, with a pistol hung low from a belt.

Then there was Horatio, the parson's son, a tall, handsome, broad-shouldered fellow of sixteen. His wheat-colored hair was combed back severely, and his face bore an expression of pain.

At the sight of these men, Punch's terror tripled.

The troupe proceeded to the church, a small, gray, wooden building with a broken thumb of a steeple. Inside it was so dark the cross itself seemed hidden. Not so much as a single picture graced the walls.

Thinking that Judy would want to be by herself, Punch began to move away, but she tugged at him and made him sit at her side in the first pew. That was pleasure.

The Merry Men sat right behind them. As for the sheriff and his pistol-packing partner, they took seats in the third row. Horatio kept to the rear.

Meanwhile, Parson Cuthwhip took his place up front, right next to Da's pine coffin, which rested bridgelike on two chairs. Then he reared back and spat out a snarling sermon about the sin of lives dedicated to frivolity. "Laughter," he stormed, "is the voice of the devil!"

Tears trickled down Judy's cheeks. Her sorrow set Punch's own grief to gush.

When the sermon was complete, the four Merry Men—all weeping jugs of water—hoisted the coffin. Punch had always thought of Mr. McSneed as a big man, but when he saw his protector's mortal remains lifted with ease, pain swelled within his chest.

The coffin, borne by the pall-bearers, left church first. Then came Parson Cuthwhip, head bowed, hands pressed together. Directly behind came Judy and Punch, followed by Sheriff Oxnard and his bearded man. Last to come was Horatio.

As they went through the door, Punch touched Judy's hand. She pushed it away. That was pain.

Outside the church they stumbled over grave mounds, avoided broken headstones, and waded through weeds until they reached the rear of the cemetery. There, a grave digger, leaning on his shovel, stood by a pile of new-dug earth and an open grave. The man's eyes showed white as snow. He was blind.

"Mr. Rockmort!" the parson bellowed to this man. "We've appeared!"

The grave digger looked up, offered a toothless grin, and shouted, "No, sir! I've no fear!" Mr. Rockmort was almost deaf, too.

The pallbearers lowered the coffin into the grave, then stepped back. Punch made a move to leave Judy's side. That time she held him close. Now Punch didn't know whether to weep from joy or sorrow.

Parson Cuthwhip turned around. Soon as he did, his pinkish face turned red. Punch looked to see the cause. Belle, having slipped her bridle, had followed and was peering over Zun's shoulder. Alexander, not to be left behind, was there, too, nose runny, grunting softly.

"I told you," the parson barked, "this is a sacred place. I want those animals removed!"

"Get them away," Judy said wearily.

Zun took hold of Belle's mane and led her beyond the cemetery fence. As for Alexander, Punch made attempts to grab him, but the pig kept darting out of reach until Punch, thoroughly winded, had to appeal to the parson.

"Pig in a service . . ." the parson snorted by way of acquiescence.

"Sit," Punch commanded.

Alexander heaved himself down by the open grave and gazed, sad-eyed, at the coffin.

With a look of disgust, the parson stepped away from the pig, clasped his hands, took a deep breath, and began: "Brethren! The wages of sin are death, and no one sins more than they who tramp the country with low animals, thieves, and medicine-show people—"

"Oh, please, sir," Judy cut in, her voice gruff with grief, "don't be mean over Da."

"I'm officiating here," the parson snarled. "This man"—he pointed into the grave—"met death to warn those of you who persist in sin."

"Begging your pardon, sir," Twig offered, hands fumbling over his derby, "but the dear departed's daughter would much prefer churchly comfort to cold chastisement."

"Hold your tongue, cur!" the parson snapped.

"Oh, sir," Judy said, her tears flowing, "in your own church you had rights to speak your faith. But if you're only going to hammer at Da's soul this way—"

"I'll speak what I want or I'll say nothing!" the parson shouted.

Judy grabbed ahold of Punch. "Let's go," she said. "We shouldn't have come."

The parson's face turned white with rage. "Sheriff Oxnard!" he shouted. "Apprehend these beggar children!"

The sheriff stepped forward. "In the name of the law," he announced, "I take you!" Even as Oxnard reached for Judy, an apple—flung by Twig—struck the sheriff's head with a *thwack!* Back he reeled. Judy and Punch began to run.

"Catch them!" Parson Cuthwhip cried. "Catch them!"

At this the sheriff's chum whipped out his pistol and began blasting the air. But Blodger, tumbler that he was, jumped onto an old gravestone, balanced for a moment, then leaped high enough so that when he landed he came down on the pistol-shooter's shoulders, sinking the bearded fellow down to his knees even as his pistol rocketed through the air.

Doc and Zun, meanwhile, heaved themselves at the sheriff.

"Help!"

Punch was almost at the gate when he heard Judy's cry. He spun about. Judy was cornered by Cuthwhip. Twig, seeing the danger, began to heave the contents of his pockets at the man. Simultaneously, Punch ripped across the cemetery and began to beat upon the parson's back and kick his shins. "Let her go!" Punch screamed. "Let her go!"

As the parson whirled to defend himself, Judy broke loose.

"Judy!" came a cry. "Here!" Horatio had led Belle into the cemetery. Judy needed no second call. Racing forward, she caught hold of Belle's mane and swung herself up. Horatio jumped out of the way.

"The children!" the parson screamed, trying to duck Twig's wooden balls, cubes, and eggs. "Stop those—" He never finished. His mouth was filled with rotten egg.

"Punch!" Judy shouted. She was urging Belle toward him.

Pursued by the egg-spitting parson, Punch scrambled forward. Judy extended her arm. Punch grabbed it and all but ran up Belle's flank. The moment he sat, Judy slapped the horse's ribs with her heels. The old mare reared. Even as she did, Parson Cuthwhip made a desperate lunge, only to be met by the horse's rump. The blow sent him staggering toward the open grave.

Alexander, who had been sitting mournfully by the grave, looked up, saw who was coming, gave a grunt, then bit the parson's ankle. Roaring with pain, the parson tried to get away. Instead, with his arms whirling like a windmill, he tottered backward, right into the grave, splitting the coffin.

Alexander peered down into the grave, gave a snuffle of satisfaction, then lumbered about. Seeing Belle—with Judy and Punch aboard—galloping through the cemetery gate, the pig streaked down the path as fast as his trotters could take him.

"Stop those men!" Parson Cuthwhip shouted from the bottom of the grave. "Stop those men!"

That was when the grave digger, Mr. Rockmort, who had been standing still as salt during the entire brawl, suddenly looked up. "Amen," he echoed, "amen!" and began to bury New Moosup's parson.

Three

With old Belle going as fast as she could gallop, Judy and Punch reached the New Moosup town line. Only then did Judy let the winded horse go at her normal plodding pace.

"Like me to get off?" Punch asked.

"Do what you want," Judy said curtly.

Stung, Punch slid down and walked by Belle's side. "Thanks for calling to me," he said, wishing Judy were not so angry.

Judy said nothing.

As they continued in a silence broken only by the clip-clop of Belle's hooves, Punch realized that this was the first time since Mr. McSneed had died that he'd been alone with Judy. He wished he knew why she had been avoiding him. Even to think about it made Punch anxious. Screwing up his courage, he said, "Judy, just before Mr. McSneed died, he called you in to him. Guess he didn't want me. You were in the wagon talking for a long time."

"I was listening."

"Well," Punch said, "you never told me what he said. Wasn't about me, was it?"

Judy frowned, shook her head, and said, "Nothing

you need to know about.'' Then she added, ''Not now.''

Frustrated, Punch glanced back over the empty road. ''Wonder where everybody is,'' he worried out loud.

''They'll be fine.''

''I'm thinking about Alexander, too.''

Judy acted as if Punch hadn't spoken.

After they had gone on for a while more, Punch tried again.

''You know who got us out, don't you?''

''The Merry Men.''

''Someone else.''

''Who?''

''Horatio. He fetched Belle. Twig says he's got eyes for you.''

Judy tossed her hair. ''I don't care,'' she said.

''You don't?''

''Only thing I'm interested in is the show,'' Judy said as she jumped off Belle and pulled off her boots.

Punch felt like saying, ''I'm glad,'' but seeing a hard look on Judy's face, he held back.

They continued on, Judy deep in thought. Then suddenly, as if reaching a decision, she said, ''Punch it's not going to be easy keeping the show together.''

''I know,'' Punch agreed.

''None of the boys will be able to do it. And Mama's so sick, I don't think she knows what's happened.''

''She'll get better,'' Punch offered. ''She has to.''

''Why?''

''With Mr. McSneed gone, she's boss.''

Judy shook her head. ''Twig is right. There's no telling if Mama will get well. So you might as well know now,'' she said. ''From now on, *I'm* boss.''

Punch stopped short. "You?" he cried, truly shocked. "But . . . what if Mrs. McSneed gets better?"

Judy put her hands on her hips and leaned in at Punch. "Punch, I *told* you, I'm going to take care of things."

"Soon as we get some audience, we'll do fine," Punch suggested, trying to push off the weight of catastrophe he felt.

Judy shook her head. "We were going bad before Da went off," she said. "It was his struggling to set us right that cast him down."

"When are you going to tell the Merry Men?"

"Soon as they get back." Then Judy said, "Twig was right too about Da saying a person's got no business having his heart in trooping unless his head is in it first."

Punch studied Judy's grief-stricken face. "Is your head in it?" he asked timidly.

Instead of answering, Judy—with tears in her eyes—strode off.

Punch hurried after her. "I just get scared," he tried to explain.

"You're always scared!"

Punch said no more.

It was only when they spied the grove of trees that marked camp that Judy looked back over the road. The Merry Men were nowhere in sight.

"Maybe they got themselves locked up," Punch suggested. "What would we do?"

"We'd get them."

"Alexander, too?" Punch asked.

"He's not worth that."

"Mr. McSneed gave him to me."

This remark brought such a look of fury to Judy's

face that Punch hastily said, "Want me to go back to town and search for everybody?"

"Punch . . ."

"What?"

"From now on, you're going to have to take care of yourself."

"But—"

"Stop asking me everything!"

Punch, finding it hard to breathe, whispered, "Do you want me to leave the show?"

"Do what you want!" she cried.

A heavy-hearted Punch turned away. When he did, he saw Alexander trotting hard up the road. Grateful for the excuse to get away, Punch hurried to greet the pig. When he got near, Alexander lay down, rolled over onto his back, and offered up his belly for a scratch. Punch flung himself down and hugged the beast. "Don't you worry," Punch whispered into Alexander's ear. "I'll never abandon *you*."

Four

When Judy and Punch reached camp, all was in confusion. Tents were flattened. Ne-Nip bottles lay helter-skelter. Costume trunks were open. And everything—clothing, wigs, shoes—was scattered.

"Mama!" Judy cried, and raced around the wagon, with Punch at her heels.

There was Mrs. McSneed—dressed in her Queen of Tipperary costume—on the wagon backboard, balanced on her belly, legs wrapped around her head, arms reaching out. She was rhythmically rocking back and forth. One hand held a pasteboard scepter, the other clutched a crystal ball. A paste-jewel crown was on her head.

The sight made Judy and Punch stand stock-still.

Suddenly Mrs. McSneed cried, "Who approaches the Queen of Tipperary?" Still rocking on her belly, her feet moved like signal flags over her head. "Speak!" she said, lifting her scepter and pointing it at Judy. "The Queen of Tipperary commands it!"

"Mama," Judy said, creeping forward. "It's me, Judy. Your daughter. Don't you know me?"

Mrs. McSneed's hands pulled back even as her legs and feet shifted forward, enabling her toes to pluck up the scepter in one foot, the ball in another. Balancing them on the soles of her feet, she stood on her hands. The crown—as it was meant to do—stayed on.

"The Queen of Tipperary has no child," she said.

"None?" Judy asked, with a sinking heart.

"We had a king who shared our throne," Mrs. McSneed proclaimed. "I've searched about, but he has fled."

"King?" Judy asked. "Who was that?"

"King Joseph McSneed."

"That's Da!" cried Punch.

Mrs. McSneed, now standing on one hand, continued: "Approach the throne and make your wishes known. But be advised, our beloved consort who shared the throne has gone." She stood on her head, legs and arms spread wide.

"Do you know where we are?" Judy asked. Her voice trembled.

"In a land where there is no laughter."

"How will you get home?"

"The king must return and bring laughter to my ear," said Mrs. McSneed, and she began to revolve slowly on her head even as one foot tossed the scepter up so that it did a complete flip in the air, landing back on her foot only to be tossed up again. Finally, she caught the scepter in her hands and, with a slow movement, set her feet behind and stood upright.

"Can we do anything for you?" Judy managed to ask.

"Bring the laughter back," Mrs. McSneed replied. And with a final flourish, she turned, opened the door at the back of the wagon, stepped inside, and closed the door behind.

"What's happened to her?" Punch implored.

Judy, face and voice heavy with woe, said, "She's gone all mad with grief."

Five

The air in the grove thickened. Afternoon shaded to dark. Judy, however, remained sitting before the wagon, staring at it, chin cupped in her hands.

Now and again, as Punch cleared up the mess that Mrs. McSneed had made, he checked the road, but saw no sign of the Merry Men, just gray storm clouds rising up beyond swaying trees. As it turned out, the men didn't appear until Punch was lighting the evening lamp.

Twig came first. His derby was dented. His coat was torn. There was a bruise on his face. Doc, who followed, not only had a puffy lip, but was sporting an eye which was turning from purple to black. Zun's clothing was torn, and he had a scratch on the side of his face, as well as a drooping mustache. Blodger held his arm as if it were broken.

Judy roused herself. "What happened?" she asked wearily.

"Ah, Judy," Twig replied, "we thought we'd done them a fare-thee-well at the cemetery. And in faith, it was a glorious battle that we won honorable. When that parson crawled out of the grave, he slunk off. But Sheriff Oxnard was loath to fly the surrender flag."

"He rounded up a score or so of healthy men," Doc added, though his cut lip made it hard for him to speak.

"Ugly, every one of them," Blodger spat out.

"You see, Judy," Twig continued, "the sheriff set up a most cowardly ambush right before the town line. Glory be! It was holy war to save our sacred liberties."

"In the dustup," Doc concluded, "we suffered serious lacerations and much bodily abuse."

Punch, getting up to fetch water, glanced toward the edges of the grove to see if the sheriff was lurking there. Just remembering the man's awful looks gave him the shudders.

The men drank the water greedily. But after that there seemed to be nothing to do but sit about in collective misery. At last Twig hauled himself up, cleared his throat, stretched his neck, grabbed his coat lapels, and said, "Fellow artists, I've come to the conclusion that we've stayed beyond our welcome here. The road calls and fortune beckons. It's time to turn our faces toward a future like we used to have."

"You're right," Doc agreed with a nod. "It's not healthy in these parts." Zun agreed. So did Blodger.

Judy looked up. "Moving," she said, "that's for me to decide."

Surprised, the bedraggled men turned around.

"What's your meaning?" Doc growled.

To which Judy replied, "I'm the new boss."

The announcement so stunned the men that no one spoke for a long time.

It was Twig who cleared his throat, rubbed his hands together, and said, "Judy, love, this decision—this becoming boss—how does that come about?"

"It's my father's show."

"Thought he died," Zun said sarcastically.

"Cost us enough," Blodger added.

Twig held up his hand to silence the others. "Your mother, dear girl," he asked in hushed tones, "has she made her last farewell?"

"She's very ill," Judy said.

"How ill?" Doc demanded.

"Not in her right mind," Judy answered. Her voice trembled.

Doc said, "What's that mean?"

"She thinks . . . she thinks she really is the Queen of Tipperary," Judy got out.

"Blessed saints . . ." Twig murmured, and crossed himself.

"So she'll not be able to take charge," Judy went on. "That leaves me as boss."

"Judy, sweet gal," Twig began with a sigh, "you know right well that it's always been me—after your da and ma—who has been number three in the local hierarchy. The wagon billing—faded though it be—reveals the truth of that. Where do you find the right to anoint yourself boss?"

"Because I'm the one to do it," Judy said. Then she added, "Anyway, that's what Da said to me before he died."

"Who else did he tell?" Doc demanded.

"My mother, I suppose," Judy replied.

"And *I'm* supposing," Twig threw in, "she's too ill to ask."

"Yes."

"Then what you're saying," Blodger interjected, "is that if we don't like the new setup, we can turn off on our own. That it?"

"That's right," Judy said.

None of the men looked directly at her. Zun kept shaking his head, while Doc stroked his beard in deep contemplation. Blodger cracked his knuckles. As for Twig, he dove into his pockets for something to juggle, but came up empty-handed.

"All right, Judy," Doc finally said, "as a measure of your practice, might I ask what you propose to do with Punch?"

Everything inside of Punch seemed to come to a halt. He dared not even draw breath.

"What about him?" Judy asked.

"Audiences are broke," Doc went on. "We need to save every penny."

"And," Blodger suggested, "Punch is as useful as a pair of boots for a fish."

"A mouth connected to a belly," Zun murmured.

"Judy," Twig pressed, "you can hear for yourself the way the boys are thinking. And you know right well the lad only stayed because of Da. So show your mettle. Cut our losses. A demonstration of strength would be most welcome."

Punch, heart thumping, legs shaking, squeezed the dollar coin that lay deep within his pocket and made a decision: If Judy agreed to what they were asking, he'd run off—instantly.

But after what seemed—to Punch—forever, Judy said, "He stays."

Weak with relief, Punch let slip his breath and glanced toward Judy. But when their eyes met he saw

41

nothing but anger, and turned away, his wretchedness renewed.

Twig looked up and around. "Is there nothing to eat?" he demanded.

Punch, grateful for the excuse, rushed to fetch the bread that was all they had for supper.

They needed to leave. Everyone knew that. Even so, sullen silence set their mood. And though the trees began to sway and thunder rumbled closer and closer, no one moved. The will to move was gone.

It was Punch, sitting apart, sharing his food with Alexander, who realized that someone was standing at the edge of the grove. "We got visitors. . . ." he whispered in alarm.

Six

Punch's words of warning made them leap up and peer into the darkness. But only when Judy hoisted the lamp did they see that it was Horatio, the parson's son, standing there with a face as pale as a winter's moon.

A nervous Twig asked, "Will you be wanting something, lad?"

Horatio opened his mouth. No words came. He swallowed hard, took a step forward, then said, "He's . . . he's planning to come after you."

"Who is?" Doc demanded.

"Sheriff Oxnard," Horatio said. "With lots more. All my father wanted to do was chase you away, but now Oxnard is swearing he's going to get hold of you if it's the last thing he does."

Punch's heart squeezed to walnut size.

"We're past the town line," Blodger protested.

"Doesn't matter," Horatio said. "He's got himself a county warrant."

Twig groaned.

"And my father," Horatio went on, "supplied him with all your names. Even the pig. You'd better get over to York State, where the warrant can't touch you."

"How far to the line?" Blodger asked.

"Maybe sixty miles."

"Take us a week!" Doc cried.

"And Oxnard," Horatio went on, "made a vow that when he does catch you, he'll make it a year in jail for whoever's your boss. And six months for the rest. He's that sore."

"When's he coming?" Judy asked.

"Three this morning," Horatio said without looking at her. "He figures you'll be sleeping."

Twig studied the young man for a moment, then said, "Well, lad, we appreciate your information regarding the way of the wind, but might there not be another bit of thought you're wanting to share?"

Horatio made a gesture that suggested he wanted to hold on to something. But when he found only air, his hand dropped. Then, in a small voice he said, "I've run away from home. I'd . . . I'd like to join you."

Doc snorted in disgust.

"Ah, boy," Twig said with a sigh, "have you any notion how many young ones have volunteered to join up with us?"

Horatio shook his head.

"This season alone the list has swollen to thirty-two!"

Blodger nodded. "I joined that way myself right after the war."

"Exactly," Doc added. "Soon as I took honors at medical school I made my practice here."

"So you see," Twig continued, "there's a touch of truth midst your father's warnings. We *are* drifters and dodgers. Put your mind to that."

"I'm willing to work," Horatio pressed, coming forward another step. "Whatever you ask."

"What about your father?" Doc demanded. "Won't he be hell-bent to haul you back?"

Horatio shook his head. "Save for preaching, he hardly ever leaves his parish."

"There's a blessing!" Zun exclaimed.

"That sheriff and his men will be quite enough," Blodger reminded them sourly.

Punch, seeing the cruel face of the sheriff in his mind, silently agreed.

"Are you the boss?" Horatio asked Twig.

"Who, me?" the old man cried with indignation. "Not on your life!" He gestured toward Judy. "She's the one."

From the moment he stepped forward, Horatio had not looked at Judy. Now, when he did, he blushed. Punch saw it.

"Can . . . can I join up?" Horatio asked Judy.

Judy turned to stare into the trees as if the answer were there.

"Please," Horatio begged. "I . . . I could be helpful."

Judy's decision took a while and when it came it was delivered in a low, nervous voice. "We'll give you a try," she said.

Even as she spoke, lightning shattered overhead and rain began to pour.

As Judy rushed inside the wagon to make sure Mrs. McSneed remained safe and dry, the rest hurried to gather up tents, pack costume trunks, and in general put equipment away. Hard enough to do by daylight, in the dark and driving rain it proved a misery. The only words Punch heard were Judy's commands as she moved about giving orders. Now and again he saw—by dim lantern light—the resentful faces of Doc and Blodger, even a clenched fist from Zun. Punch kept wondering what he'd do if fists were more than shaken. But nothing did occur.

As for Horatio, who worked extra hard, Punch sensed how fearful he was that if they did not clear our fast, Sheriff Oxnard would show up and drag him home. Punch couldn't help noticing how quick and strong the young man was and how, in comparison, he himself only did half as much or as well. Worst of all, Punch kept seeing Judy steal glances in Horatio's direction. It set Punch to wondering what she really thought of this parson's son.

Seven

In the two hours it took to get ready, the torrential rain turned the grove into a bog. The old wagon had so many things heaped upon it that it looked like a pincushion on wheels. It took everyone pushing and pulling—plus Belle between the wagon shafts—to roll it onto the muddy road. Then, soaking wet and slathered with mud, the troupe gathered around the sputtering lamp and tried to decide which way to go.

Judy shoved wet hair from her face and shouted over the pelting rain to ask Horatio if the sheriff would be coming directly from town.

"Said he would," was the reply.

"This road runs east and west," Judy pointed out. "Any way to get around them, like going north or south?"

"I've never traveled that far," Horatio confessed. "But I think there's a logging road back east a mile. It's supposed to run north maybe five miles."

Zun shook his head. "York State is west!" he objected.

"The sheriff will be coming from that way," Judy reminded him.

Zun gave her a sour look.

"We have to go around," Judy said. "Any other roads along that way you mentioned?" she asked Horatio.

"I think there's a post road which links up to the turnpike," he said. "It runs northwest."

"A good road?" Blodger demanded.

Horatio said, "Never been on it."

"We don't have much choice!" Judy declared. "We'll go that way. Just find the post road," she told Horatio.

Off they set, Horatio leading the way. Twig stayed by his side, holding up the lamp. Then came Zun, guiding Belle and the wagon. The rest slipped and slopped along the clotted road as best they could. Time and again they had to haul the wagon out of the mud. All the while the storm went on.

When Horatio finally found the post road, it was long past midnight. Twig held up the lamp for a look. What they saw was little more than a path, more mucked and mangled than the road on which they had been traveling. But there was little choice. They moved in the new direction. It was not until four in the morning that Judy allowed them to stop.

She herself disappeared into the wagon with her mother. As for the exhausted men, instead of setting up tents, each one took a bit of canvas and stumbled into the woods. After finding a bit of high ground, they wrapped canvas about themselves and, cocoon-like, lay down to sleep.

Though exhausted, Punch could not rest. The funeral—Judy's anger, followed by her kindness—the feelings the Merry Men had shown for him—Horatio's arrival—he was certain it was only a matter of days before Judy sent him away. Why else had she been willing to let Horatio join except to replace him?

Punch tried but could not even begin to guess where he'd go or what would happen to him. "If I do go," he whispered to Alexander, who slept by his side, "I'll take you."

When Punch finally fell into a fitful doze, he was soon awakened by a sound. Fearful that Sheriff Oxnard was bursting upon them, Punch sat up and listened tensely. All he could hear, however, was rain dripping through the sodden trees.

Nervously, Punch poked his head out from beneath his canvas and looked about. By the light of the hooded lamp Judy had left on, he made out the wagon. The sound was coming from there. Telling Alexander to stay, Punch quietly made his way toward it. The cold, wet earth made him shiver.

Only when he drew close to the wagon did he see the source of the noise. Mrs. McSneed, dressed in her queen's costume, was standing on her head.

Punch slipped behind some trees. In moments Judy appeared and, talking soothingly, led her mother back inside the wagon. Moments later Judy returned, leaned against the wagon, and just stood there, her face soaked with rain and sorrow.

Punch watched. He wanted to step forward, to talk to Judy, to comfort her. But scared of what she might say, fearful of arousing her anger, he crept back to the canvas.

Feeling useless and full of shame, Punch hugged Alexander and cried himself to sleep.

Eight

By morning the rain had turned to heavy mist. Alexander was gone, rooting, Punch figured, for food in the woods. For a while Punch stayed under cover, thinking about what he had seen the night before. He had just about made up his mind that he would have to beg Judy to be allowed to stay when a sniff told him Doc's breakfast concoction was at the boil.

"You're late," snapped Doc when he appeared. "Fetch the bowls."

Punch passed the breakfast around. When he handed a bowl to Zun, it slipped. Food splashed to the ground.

"Clumsy fool!" Zun raged.

Blodger looked around. "Folks who spill soup soon steal bread," he said.

Half an hour later, Judy joined the group. To Punch she looked worn out. All the same she said, "We better start soon. The York line is a long way off. That sheriff might be following."

"Oxnard won't give up easy," Horatio agreed.

As quickly as possible they set off. Overhead the sky was gray and hot. Below, mud sucked at their heels. The heat made them sweat. And with every step they took, mosquitoes stung and gnats swarmed.

Horatio went along with Punch.

"Is the going usually this rough?" Horatio asked.

"Not always," replied Punch, who now had to skip to keep up with the young man's longer strides.

"We'll be stopping to perform soon, won't we?"

"Ask Judy. She's in charge."

"You her brother?" Horatio asked abruptly.

The notion pleased Punch, but he shook his head. "Da—Mr. McSneed, that is—he found me. Wanted me to stay."

"How come?"

Punch gave the only answer he'd ever been able to come up with: "He needed a servant."

"Must be fine being on your own this way," Horatio enthused. "No one telling you what to do or think. Say, is that Pudlow a real doctor?"

"No."

"But Mr. Zunbadden, he's a true count, isn't he?"

"Born in Brooklyn, New York."

Horatio thought for a moment. "What about Blodger, then? Where's he from?"

"Woonsocket, Rhode Island."

Horatio considered, then said, "What's your job with the show?"

"Whatever they ask."

"Anything in particular you perform?"

"Not me."

"How come?"

"Told you. I'm just company servant."

Horatio grinned. "If you're a servant, you're lucky they keep you. I saw you drop that food at breakfast."

"I know," Punch mumbled, and stopped trying to keep up.

It was midafternoon when they got out of the woods.

They had no idea where they were, not even which way they were heading. Seeing a house, Judy decided to ask for directions.

When she asked Punch to go with her, he was pleased. But as they walked up the rutted path to the house, she said, "I saw you sneaking about when Mama came out last night."

Punch, caught off guard, kept his eyes on the path.

"She's none of your business," Judy warned.

"Just wanted to help," Punch managed to say.

"She doesn't like you. Never has."

Punch would have given anything to know if that was Judy's feeling consisted too, but he didn't dare ask.

They reached the house. It was hardly more than a shack, with paint peeling off in long curls like a gift someone had begun to open, only to change their mind when they guessed what was inside.

At the door, a gray-haired woman in a sack dress appeared. Two sloe-eyed, slack-jawed children with dirty undershirts and no pants clung to her legs.

Judy explained to the woman that they were trying to get to the York State line.

"Well, dearie," the woman said, her tone acid, "you're going about it wrong. Your wagon's pointed east, and you need to head west."

Judy sighed. "Is there a town nearby?" she asked.

"Bigalow, three miles west."

"How are things there?"

"Like everywhere else, sorrowful bad."

"What did the woman say?" Blodger demanded when Judy and Punch got back.

"We've been heading the wrong way," she said.

Doc let forth a streak of swearing.

"But there's a town three miles away," Judy informed them. "It's called Bigalow. Anyone know it?"
No one did.

"Maybe we can perform there," Judy said.

It was even hotter and more humid when they came over a hill and saw the small town of Bigalow below. Set beside a muddy river, it had a still, sour look.

"The fair city of Bigalow!" Doc cried sarcastically. "The heart of the nation! The center of civilization! The core of the universe! Bigalow, we have arrived!"

Judy sent Twig into town while Blodger and Doc went off, sacks in hand, to search for food and Ne-Nip makings. Zun told Punch what he wanted done with Belle. Horatio, meanwhile, unloaded equipment and laid things out to dry. Punch helped there, too. He also got a fire going and lined up empty Ne-Nip bottles. Judy, meanwhile, took care of Mrs. McSneed.

When Doc and Blodger came back, their sacks were full of greens. Doc called to Punch for help, and they set about working his Ne-Nip mix, which consisted of grass, water, and whatever Doc threw in.

It was dark when Twig returned from Bigalow. "It's your regular mill town," he informed them. "But the mill's shut tighter than a banker's wallet and people are looking poor as pups without a ma."

Glancing up from his brew, Doc said, "Medically speaking, money is the only thing that'll cure us."

"There's a common where we can play," Twig allowed.

"Will they let us use it?" Blodger asked.

"Doubt they care a flea's finger if we do or don't."

"How far are we from New Moosup?" Zun asked.

"Six miles."

"Only six!" Judy cried.

Horatio turned chalky white.

"What about that sheriff?" Blodger wanted to know. "Any sign of him?"

"Not yet," Twig said.

"If that sheriff *is* coming after us," Blodger warned, "and we stop here, we'll be giving him more time to find us."

"But Doc's right," Judy said. "We need money. So we'll perform tomorrow."

In the evening, when Punch had cleaned up dinner and was sitting out with Alexander, Horatio approached him. He squatted down, picked up a twig, and begun to pluck at it.

"Say, Punch," he said after a spell, "what happens during a performance?"

Punch explained: "First we march to town. That gets us our audience. Then we'll head for the common. When we get there, I'll set out the ring. They do the show in that. I work that, too. Then, after we've done the whole thing, Doc makes his Ne-Nip pitch, which is when we make our money. In the end I collect equipment, load up, and we all come back to camp.''

"What am I supposed to do?"

Punch shrugged. "You'll have to ask Judy."

Horatio was still for a moment, then he said, "That Judy, she's pretty nice."

Punch was silent.

"I know you're not in the running," Horatio went on, his voice low and confidential. "But what about others? She have a sweetheart anywhere?"

Punch's hand trembled. "I don't figure so," he said.

"What do you say?" Horatio asked. "Think I've got a chance?"

Punch stole a look at Horatio's face and couldn't help but wonder if he would ever be so tall or so good-looking. "I suppose," he finally answered.

"That your pig?"

"Yes."

"Got a name?"

"Alexander."

"Come winter," Horatio said, "he'll be good eating."

When Punch shut his eyes and said nothing, Horatio laughed, got up, and moved away. Punch watched as he went over to where Judy was sitting by the wagon. Soon the two were deep in conversation.

"Come on," Punch said to Alexander. "Let's take a walk."

Alexander and Punch strolled through a meadow. "I saw a strong man, once," Punch said to the pig. "He lifted four hundred pounds. Alexander, you should have seen him. His partner challenged anybody to lift more than the strong man. No one could. So people just stood around and admired him. Wish I could be like that."

Alexander paid no mind.

That night, when the rest were asleep, Punch stayed awake in a place where he could watch the wagon without being seen. It was near midnight when Mrs. McSneed came out of the wagon and began to do her act. Judy soon emerged. Mrs. McSneed spoke just as if she really were a queen, and Judy answered as her subject.

Heart pounding, Punch crept up and stood near. Judy noticed him and frowned, but said nothing, just turned and kept watch on her mother. Mrs. McSneed was spinning on her head.

"Please," Punch whispered, "let me help."

"No," Judy said.

"I could stay while you get some sleep."

"Mama's never liked you."

"But what's going to happen to her when we're performing?" Punch asked. Mrs. McSneed was standing on one hand, twirling her scepter with a foot.

"She'll stay in the wagon," Judy said. "Horatio will guard her."

"*Horatio?*"

"She seems to like him."

"But . . ."

"Punch, you either do as I tell you, or . . ."

Punch's heart seemed to stumble. "Or . . . what?"

Judy started to speak, checked herself, and only shook her head. "Just go back to sleep," she said.

When Punch crawled into his tent, Alexander grunted a greeting. A grateful Punch flung his arms around the pig's neck, then tried to think about the next day's show. Would it, he kept asking himself, be his last?

Nine

It made no difference that Punch wished the next day would not come. As scheduled, it arrived. And that afternoon "Joe McSneed and His Merry Men" marched into the town of Bigalow.

First in line came Twig. He had on his multipocketed plaid coat with his brown derby set cockeyed on his head. As he high-stepped along, he juggled three bottles of Ne-Nip.

Next came Blodger, wearing blue tights held up by pink suspenders. His shirt was faded scarlet. A big bass drum was strapped to his chest and, despite his sore arm, he thumped away like the Lord's own heart.

Behind Blodger came Zun, his outfit consisting of red trousers, a gray army jacket, and a helmet set off by tattered ostrich feathers. His mustache, waxed and twirled, stuck our fiercely. He sported a cornet.

By Zun's side strode Doc, all fancy—despite his black eye—in fine dinner jacket, striped trousers, and top hat. He had brushed his white beard, parted it in two, and tied one half with red ribbon, the other half with green. He carried a tambourine.

Punch, as usual, came behind the Merry Men. He wore no costume, just his regular patched overalls and bare feet. But Alexander, trotting by his side, wore a yellow bonnet.

Punch was leading Belle by her bridle. The old horse had her swayback draped in a threadbare, baby-blue blanket.

Standing on Belle was Judy. She wore a green tutu, hem aslant. Above her fluffed red hair and freckled face perched a pointed hat that trailed a tattered yellow veil. She was trying to smile, but Punch could see it did not come easy.

Belle pulled the wagon, which carried the performance equipment. Inside, Horatio kept watch over a sleeping Mrs. McSneed.

When the troupe marched into Bigalow, Blodger began beating his drum loudly, Doc shook out a tambourine echo, and Zun set to blowing a squeaky cornet song with a tempo all its own.

The music pulled Bigalow's children onto the streets. Their clothing might have been ragged, their faces none too clean, but they were excited by what they saw and heard. They skipped, jumped, and tagged along. And as the parade passed on, more people followed, each new wave slightly older than the last.

But as "Joe McSneed and His Merry Men" marched along the muddy streets of town, Punch noticed that the Grand Hotel was closed, the Bank of Commerce was windowless, the People's General Store was no more, and a farmer's feed store had failed. The only thing that seemed afloat was the Grand Salvation Saloon.

Twig was supposed to lead the way—and the trailing audience—to the common. But Bigalow was none too regular. The old man led them into a dead-end alley, which required a general retreat. Only by Blodger shout-

ing "Right!" and "Left!" at Twig did they finally reach the common.

Once there, Twig aimed for the band platform. But when the troupe attempted to follow, the wagon sank axle-deep in mud. Townspeople, eager to help, swarmed in and worked so hard to free the wagon that Punch grew fearful their shouting would arouse Mrs. McSneed.

Trying to move the wagon proved useless. It only went from mudhole to mudhole. Judy decided they'd perform right where they were. Punch did not even set out the ring.

So it was that Twig, serving as master of ceremonies—Da's old job—stood within the muddy semicircle before the wagon and faced an audience of fifty. Half the audience were children. Another quarter were grayheads. Three were lame veterans. The rest were old enough to have money—but tattered clothing suggested otherwise. Worst of all—to Punch's eyes—every face seemed set in stone.

"Ladies and gentlemen of the fair city of Bigalow," Twig shouted, making big gestures as he began. "It's my singular privilege to be presenting 'Joe McSneed and His Merry Men!' We've been traveling many a mile to be here with you this darling summer day! For your pleasure we'll be performing acts previously seen only by crowned heads of Europe. To be sure, here in republican America you'll be equally beguiled and bedazzled. We have music, thrills, and legerdemain! And, at the conclusion of the performance, when I pass my hat, we'll be hoping you'll make your own contribution to our life, liberty, and particular pursuit of happiness.

"Finally, as a special attraction—but only at the ultimate conclusion—you'll be meeting his high and mighty, the famous Dr. F. X. Pudlow, and his truly miraculous Ne-Nip. Ne-Nip's a drink that's guaranteed to cure whatever turns you poor or sulky! Taken from the secret recipes of ancients! And I'm telling you true, it's sweet as poteen and twice as potent!

"And now, for your pleasure, I'll perform an exhibition of fantastical juggling!"

That was Zun's cue for stepping out from behind the wagon, lifting cornet to his lips, and playing a waltz, which he did in his own sour fashion. At the same time Twig reached into his pockets and extracted three bottles of Ne-Nip. These he began to juggle, now and again salting his act by mugging at the audience. The audience, however, seemed to be asleep.

Twig, trying to wake them up, worked harder by reaching into a pocket and adding another bottle to his juggle. Still, the audience showed no emotion. Then five bottles were going through the air. Six!

Punch, looking on, began to wonder if the audience had eyes to see.

Growing desperate, Twig fetched up an apple and put that into his mix. A cube of wood. An egg. The audience barely blinked. And the faster Twig worked, the whiter grew his face until—bled of energy by the unresponsive audience—he abruptly stopped, gathered in his things, and marched off behind the wagon, muttering, "Toads, maggots . . ." under his breath.

Zun, caught by surprise, cut short his playing and hurried off, too.

A few people in the audience clapped a hand or two. A few booed. Some, however, left entirely.

Punch hurried out from behind the wagon and set a half barrel into the mud, then ran back. It was time for Doc.

"Ladies and gentlemen," the bandy-legged fellow cried as he shook his tambourine, "we're proud to present Count Gustav Zunbadden and his wonder horse, Belle. Count Zunbadden has just arrived from Russia to perform. Above all, please note that upon Belle's back is—Zoralinda, the Queen of Tipperary's favorite daughter, who performs unequal acts of equestrian elegance!"

At that, Zun, mustache ends turned down fiercely, came out from behind the wagon, leading Belle. On Belle's back stood Judy.

Zun guided Belle in a muddy, clumsy prance around the barrel, moving to Doc's tambourine beat. Judy, meanwhile, stood up and extended her arms to either side. On her face was a smile as frozen as the North Pole. In each hand she held a Ne-Nip bottle.

A second circle was completed with Judy standing on one foot. Then Zun had Belle turn to face the crowd.

"How does zee feel?" Zun asked Belle with an accented voice. Belle bobbed her head up and down. "Bravo!" Zun cried. "She knows zee answer!"

Doc, trying to milk applause, shook the tambourine. Someone in the audience clapped. But more left.

Next Zun had Belle trot about the central barrel. While the horse was doing this, Judy performed a jig on her back. The dance consisted of hopping from one foot to another—all the while smiling broadly—even as she swung one arm behind her back, one forward.

Judy's jig was Punch's favorite moment. It was when he thought Judy most beautiful. But the remaining audience was unimpressed.

For a climax Zun led Belle to the half barrel. There he had the old horse step up with her two front legs. As she did, Judy did her final flourish, standing on two hands while Belle lifted a foreleg. Doc, meanwhile, shook his tambourine furiously.

"Thank yous! Thank yous!" Zun bellowed.

There was some mild applause as Zun led Belle and Judy off. But even more people left.

Once again Twig came out from behind the wagon.

"My friends!" he cried. "We're delighted to present for your enthusiastic response an act of balance and restraint never seen, imagined, or even contemplated in our entire world. It's my pleasure to present Boldger, the African acrobat!"

Punch sloshed his way through the mud to set up two posts fifteen feet apart. Then he slung a rope, three feet above the ground, from one post to the other. Once the posts were set, Punch hauled back on one of them, while Twig pulled back on the other, making the rope between taut. That done, Doc began to smack his tambourine as Blodger emerged, ready to walk the rope.

The first thing Blodger did was greet the audience with a halfhearted salute and grim smile. Then he tested the rope. After that he clambered up to—and over—Punch's back, so as to step on the rope. With arms stretched to either side, he walked the length of the rope, turned about and walked back, jumped down to the mud, and bowed.

The audience offered no reaction at all.

With a grunt of annoyance, Blodger went back on the rope, walked to its middle, turned around, faced first one way, then another. Again he bowed to the audience. Again there was no response.

At that Blodger jumped off the rope and walked away in disgust. Three children clapped. But six more people, all adults, left.

For Punch and Twig, there was nothing to do except remove the rope.

Zun made the next presentation. "We shall set in front of zee," he cried out, "a ting that has baffled all tinkers of the universe. A fabulous act."

Blodger and Punch, both wearing large, flowing black capes, carried out what was known as Doc's Disappearing Box. This was a wooden box, three square feet. As they set it down, Doc came out from behind the wagon and bowed.

"Ladies and gentlemen," he began. "You see this box. It's made of good wood." He rapped it. "True, it's not as solid as this boy's head." He rapped Punch's head. "See? But this box has a lid. Assistants, lift the lid."

Punch lifted it.

"As you can observe, it's empty. Lower it."

Punch lowered it.

"Now," Doc continued, "I'll stand on the box." He did. "My assistants will now place a curtain around me."

Blodger and Punch lifted a barrel hoop, to which a dark cloth had been attached, over Doc's head. When they lowered the cloth, it covered him completely.

"Drop the hoop," Doc cried from inside the drapery.

The cloth was lowered. There stood Doc.

"Now, then," Doc called, producing a bottle of Ne-Nip from a pocket. "I'll demonstrate how good one bottle of Ne-Nip is for making all ailments vanish!"

With a flourish he opened the bottle and pretended to drink down the contents. "Lift the hoop!" he ordered.

Once again Doc was hidden from view.

"Drop it!" came the command. Blodger and Punch did nothing. "Did you not hear me?" Doc yelled. "Drop it!" That time, when they dropped the curtain, Doc was not there.

The remaining audience—only half the number of those at the beginning—was truly surprised. Some real applause rang out. Then, as always happened, a child in the audience called, "He's in the box!"

"What?" Blodger said, stepping forward even as Punch began to move backward toward the wagon. Doc was behind Punch, hiding under his cape.

"He's in the box!" the child yelled. Others took up the call.

"I don't hear you!" Blodger shouted, coming forward so that the audience would keep their eyes on him. At the same time, Punch was backing up against the wagon so Doc could slip away.

"He's in the box," the calls insisted.

"Oh," said Blodger, as if just understanding. "You want to see what's inside the box!" Slowly, he stepped back, tilted the box up and opened it, showing it to be empty. The crowd, once again surprised, applauded.

"Here I am!" came a cry. Atop the wagon stood Doc, bottles of Ne-Nip in each hand. "You see," he cried. "Ne-Nip makes things disappear!

"But now," he exclaimed, "I have the honor of offering—at a very special low price—to each and every one of you, the miracle of Ne-Nip, the ancient drink from the pyramids, which cures whatever ails you. It—"

At that moment the rear door of the wagon flung

open with a bang. Mrs. McSneed, dressed in her queen's costume, appeared. She was walking on her hands.

The audience blinked.

Horatio tried to grab the woman, but Mrs. McSneed was too quick. She hopped to the ground, sank wrist-deep into mud, then waddled over to Doc's box and climbed upon it. From her upside-down position she examined the crowd. The audience, bewildered, stared back.

"I am the banished Queen of Tipperary!" Mrs. McSneed proclaimed. "Where is the laughter? Where is it?"

A look of horror on his face, Blodger backed away. That left Punch alone with Mrs. McSneed.

Punch, very frightened, tried desperately to think what to do. The first thing he did was step in front of Mrs. McSneed to shield her from the audience.

Mrs. McSneed peered at him. "You're not the king!" she cried. "Be gone!"

Punch glanced at the wagon in hopes that someone would come to the rescue. No one came. He turned back to the audience, which was staring fixedly at him, as though waiting for *him* to act. And indeed, he kept saying to himself, Do something to distract the audience!

It was then—without further thought—that Punch began to jig. The jig was perhaps half the one he had danced for Mr. McSneed four years before. The other half was a crude imitation of what Judy performed atop Belle's back, a limping hop from foot to foot with some random swinging of arms. He also flung his hands wide, splayed his fingers, twitched his shoulders, and rolled his eyes. All the while he tried to smile, though it was not joy he was feeling, but panic. The whole effect was rather like a broken rag doll hung from a twisted spring, bounced by a clumsy child.

The audience, however, began to giggle. The giggling convinced Punch he was doing something wrong. Not knowing whom else to call upon, he yelled, "Alexander! Alexander!"

Alexander, wearing his sunbonnet, scrambled out from beneath the wagon, trotted over, and blinked up at his friend.

Mrs. McSneed, still standing on her hands atop Doc's box, saw Alexander. "He's not the king!" she cried.

That time the audience laughed out loud.

The laughter, as unexpected as it was unwanted, frightened Punch anew. He bent over, grasped Alexander's front legs, and hoisted him up. Then he began to sway back and forth as if he and the pig were dancing. Alexander licked his face. The audience howled with glee. Some even clapped their hands. Punch, increasingly terrified, began to caper up and down with Alexander until Judy finally came out. She took a firm hold of her mother and led her behind the wagon. As they went, Mrs. McSneed kept calling, "Was that my king? Was that my king?"

The audience roared.

The moment Punch saw Mrs. McSneed safely stowed, he stopped his dance. And the audience also ceased to laugh.

Doc, who had never left his perch atop the wagon, now called out, "Ladies and gentlemen. May I have your attention here, please! Once again I wish to offer— at a special low, low price of twenty-five cents—the miracle of Ne-Nip, which will cure whatever ails you."

That day he sold two bottles of Ne-Nip. And when Twig passed the hat, they collected only thirty-seven cents.

Ten

Upset by the small collections as well as by Mrs. McSneed's appearance, the troupe retreated to camp in sullen silence. Punch, trailing behind the rest, kept wishing he had been able to think of something else to do—other than dance—when Mrs. McSneed appeared. He knew his performance had been a dreadful thing. Oh, why hadn't anyone else *done* something? As soon as they got back to camp, he stayed out of sight.

Around the camp fire that night there was little talk. Judy stayed in the wagon. Punch, who assumed she did so out of anger, felt only worse. Then, when he handed Blodger his bowl of stew, the acrobat sniffed and said, "You're the fool, going out and imitating Judy. You're the reason we took in so little."

Punch hung his head. "I didn't know what else to do," he explained.

"Making fun of Judy," Zun sneered with a shake of his head, "the one person who keeps you around."

"If I were to give a medical opinion," Doc added, "I'd say it proves you're an idiot!"

"Ah, Punch," Twig said knowingly, "sure as certain Judy has come to her senses and will toss you now. If you had half a heart, you'd haul yourself away before she slings your slog.''

When dinner was done and a mournful Punch was cleaning up, he looked on as the four men went off together and talked, keeping their voices low. Then he watched as Horatio ambled over to the wagon and knocked on the rear door. Judy poked out her head. When she saw it was Horatio, she let him come in.

Punch finished his chores. Then he called up Alexander, and the two went for a stroll. Punch decided Twig was right. It was inevitable that Judy would ask him to leave. Maybe that very night. Just the thought so frightened Punch, he decided he must at least try and apologize to Judy. He wondered if he could humble himself enough that she might allow him to stay a bit.

"Alexander," Punch said. The pig looked up. "Would you mind if I practiced making my apology to you?"

Alexander gave a grunt.

"Sit, please," Punch requested. The pig did. Punch gazed into his face. "I'm awful sorry I did what I did," he began. "Can you find it in your heart to forgive me? I mean, I didn't mean to mock you. I didn't!" At that Punch threw himself on his knees and, clasping his hands, cried, "Oh, Judy, you know how much I love you!"

When Alexander leaned in to lick his face, Punch burst into tears.

That night Punch was too anxious to sleep. Instead, he crawled out of his tent and made his way toward the wagon. Drawing close, he saw Judy sitting on the backboard. He started to go forward, prepared to apologize. Then he realized that Horatio was sitting right next to her. The two were holding hands.

Punch gazed at them for a while, then retreated sadly to his tent.

Next morning Judy announced that they would not do a second performance in Bigalow. "There's no money there," she said. Then she said, "Punch, I need to talk to you."

"Now you'll get it," Doc hissed, loud enough for the others to hear. Twig giggled, while Blodger muttered, "Amen." Zun snatched up his cornet and played a mournful "taps."

Trembling with fear, Punch followed Judy around the wagon. Then he waited, head down, for the worst.

Eleven

"Look here," Judy said to Punch when they were alone, "I need you to go to Bigalow. Find out the best way to the York State border. Can you do that?"

Punch looked up in surprise. *"Me?"* he said.

"Yes, you."

"But . . . why not Twig? Or Blodger?"

"I don't trust them."

"You don't?"

"Punch, can you do what I'm asking or not?"

"I—I think so," Punch stammered.

"Just make sure you find a way that avoids New Moosup. Go on now."

Punch, eyes cast down, remained where he was.

"What's the matter?" Judy asked.

"I'm—I'm sorry about yesterday," Punch blurted out.

"What are you talking about?" Judy demanded.

"You know . . . when Mrs. McSneed . . . I mean, I wasn't intending to make fun of her . . . or you."

"The audience seemed to like it," Judy said coolly.

"I'm just sorry," Punch repeated, then turned and fled into Bigalow, feeling that in some way—he didn't know how—he was reprieved.

In town Punch searched for a young person to talk to. It didn't take long before he found a few children sitting on the front steps of a house. He explained his need for directions.

"Head over to that stable," a girl suggested as she pointed the way, "and ask for Fat Boy. He knows the roads." The other kids grinned and agreed. "Remember, ask for Fat Boy."

Punch went to the stable pointed out and found a squat, fat boy in gray overalls cleaning muck boxes. He was smoking a pipe. Punch watched him for a while. Then he said, "Are you Fat Boy?"

Instantly, the boy whirled and set his pitchfork against Punch's chest. "You looking to see your guts?" he snarled. Smoke poured from his pipe.

"No . . ." Punch said, backing up in haste.

"Don't call me that name."

"Well . . ." Punch sputtered. "What should I call you?"

"My name! Percival!"

"Per-Percival, can I ask you something?"

"No harm to the ask-ing," Percival snarled, only to suddenly lower his fork and grin. "Say, I know you," he said, his tone completely altered.

"You do?"

"Sure. Yesterday, you were dancing with that pig, right? You were as funny as all get-out."

"I was?"

"Saving you," Percival said, "the rest was bunk. What's your name?"

"Punch."

"Punch. I like that. Want a smoke?" He held out his pipe. "No corn silk or junk. Real 'bacco."

Punch shook his head.

"You going to do that again around here?" Percival asked.

"No."

"You been traveling with them folks long?"

"Some . . ."

"Say, Punch, you ever see a lion?"

Again Punch shook his head.

"Well, I did. About a year ago," Percival went on, "the Clodbarken Family Circus came in here. You ever hear of them?"

Punch shook his head.

"Them Clodbarkens had a lion. Pretty swell, though it had no teeth to speak of. Hey, there was a sheriff asking for you people," Percival said.

Punch's heart gave a thump. "A sheriff?"

"Fellow from over around New Moosup way. Sheriff Oxnard."

"When?" Punch's voice shook.

"This morning. Early." Percival nodded to one of the stable stalls. "That's his horse right there. And I can tell you, the horse is a lot better-looking than he is, that end anyway."

"What did he want?" Punch found voice to ask.

"Didn't say exactly. Just wanted to know if you folks had passed through."

"You tell him?"

"Not me. When a mean one goes looking for a circus, it's not likely he's looking for laughs."

"Do you know the best way to get to the York State border?" Punch asked hastily.

"That where you going?"

"Maybe," Punch said, trying to avoid Percival's grin.

"Can't say I blame you," Percival offered with a wink. "Sure you don't want a smoke?"

When Punch declined again, Percival gave directions to the state line, and Punch thanked him. As he left, Percival called, "Say, Punch, you get into trouble you come on back. Just ask for Fat Boy."

"The border isn't easy to get to," Punch reported when he returned to camp, and he gave the directions Percival had provided.

"How many miles?" Twig wanted to know.

"I didn't ask."

"You might have," Doc snapped.

"There's another thing," Punch said. "This morning Sheriff Oxnard was in town looking for us."

"Blessed saints . . ." murmured Twig. "He *is* coming after us."

"Did anyone say anything about the show?" Judy asked.

"No," Punch lied, not wanting to make Judy feel bad by repeating Fat Boy's words.

"We better move on," Judy said.

Twelve

By the next afternoon "Joe McSneed and His Merry Men" reached the town of Portree, only to find it more or less deserted. When Judy inquired why, she was told that a prayer meeting was in progress.

"Who's conducting it?" she asked quickly.

"Fellow up from over New Moosup way. Parson Brutus Cuthwhip."

The troupe scrambled to get away, not stopping until midnight. Next day they marched to the town of Snarburg, where they performed before an audience of eleven. The acts did go better than at Bigalow. But Doc was only able to sell one bottle of Ne-Nip. And when Twig sent around his derby, the collection amounted to fifteen cents.

Before the performance Judy had bolted the wagon door so Mrs. McSneed would not be able to get out. Even so, Punch was sure he heard the door rattle. Fortunately, the lock held.

In camp that night, when Punch came out of his tent and made his way toward the wagon, Horatio loomed up and blocked his way.

"Where do you think you're going?" he demanded.

"To the wagon," Punch managed to say.

"What for?"

"To help Judy."

"Look here," Horatio informed him. "Judy doesn't want your help. You know she's told you so. Now get on back where you belong."

Punch, deeply hurt, slunk away.

All the next day they traveled, finally reaching the town of Sparkle, population twenty-seven. Judy said they had to perform. The collection came to five cents.

After dinner, when Punch was washing out the bowls in the stream near where they had camped, he noticed Doc and Blodger hunkered off together, their voices low. By taking careful steps and staying hidden, Punch crept close enough to hear their talk without being seen.

". . . she can't do it," Blodger was saying. "Judy just don't know how."

"As a medical man," Doc said, "my opinion is that we shouldn't have let her be boss, that's all."

To this Blodger nodded and added, "It's all downhill and smash."

"Not with me," Doc returned with anger. "I'll jump before that. You can count on me."

Punch stole away. "Trouble's coming," he confided to Alexander.

From Sparkle the troupe moved west until an impassable road forced them south, after which they went north again, where they came upon the town of Hazen. Hazen claimed 422 residents.

Zun and Twig scouted the place. When they returned, Twig was full of doubts.

"Judy, it's no good," he warned, wringing his derby in his hands. "No one's had a job there for seven months."

"Sullen as empty socks," Zun agreed.

"We need money," Judy said. "We'll just have to chance it."

Before the performance Judy once again locked Mrs. McSneed in the wagon. Judy also decided it was time for Horatio to help work the show. "It'll make things go smoother," she informed Punch.

"And maybe better," Horatio added with a grin.

Punch, certain this was yet another step in Judy's preparations to get rid of him, said nothing.

Judy put Horatio into a costume of baggy green pants, an oversize yellow jacket, and a hat that pulled over his eyes.

"Don't I look silly?" Horatio protested, clearly uncomfortable.

"You wanted to join us," Judy chided him. Her tone pleased Punch.

The weather that late afternoon was dull, with thick, cool air and a mottled sky. They marched through town, drew a crowd, and set up on the common. Twig gave the opening speech and then began his juggle. Right from the start the audience began to hiss.

Judy, looking on from near the wagon, whispered, "Get him off!" into Punch's ear and pushed him forward.

Punch approached the old man timidly. "Judy said you should come off." He tried to keep his voice low.

Twig, ignoring Punch, continued to juggle. Helpless, Punch looked to Judy.

"Off!" she insisted.

That time Punch took hold of Twig's arm. The old man, caught off guard, looked around. Seeing Punch, he became angry and tried to hit the boy, but missed. The force of his swing, however, spun him around so that he tripped and fell on the ground.

That, the audience found amusing.

In despair Punch appealed to Judy again. She sent Horatio out. With Punch taking Twig by one arm, Horatio the other, they dragged him off.

"A scandal!" Twig cried even as they pulled him away. "A great scandal is taking place!"

The audience jeered.

Doc came forward and introduced Zun and Judy. Zun emerged on cue, but Judy, distracted by what had happened to Twig, had not set herself properly on Belle's back. When the old horse stepped forward, she slipped off. Zun, not noticing, continued to lead Belle around the ring while Judy, hitching up her tutu, had to run to catch up, her veil streaming behind her.

The audience started to boo.

Not understanding what was happening, Zun stopped and scowled at the crowd. The audience answered with more booing.

Judy, face flushed red, clambered onto Belle's back. "It's all right," she appealed to Zun. "Pay no mind! Go on!"

But Zun, full of fury, continued to look at the crowd with anger. The crowd, sensing it was they who were making him mad, and enjoying it, yelled even more. Exasperated, Zun made a rude gesture. The audience, turning hostile, started to whistle and mock.

"Go on!" Judy pleaded to Zun. "Ignore them!"

Zun decided he'd had enough. He marched out of the ring, leaving Judy alone with Belle. There was nothing for Judy to do but stand on Belle's back and do as poky a jig as ever she danced.

The audience began to mock even more until Horatio put an end to Judy's act by rushing out and leading Belle away.

Once behind the wagon, a livid Judy leaped off Belle and searched for Zun. When she saw him, he was storming off the common.

"Stop the show!" she ordered.

Even as she gave her orders, there came the sound of splintering wood. The next moment, the wagon locks gave way and the door burst open. Out popped Mrs. McSneed—on her hands. Dressed in her queen's costume, she minced to the edge of the backboard, then did a back flip, landing on her feet. Then she folded back upon herself and stood on her hands again. Her dress flowed down, revealing red bloomers. That caused a ruckus in the audience.

Mrs. McSneed—her head hidden beneath her skirts— began to hand-walk toward the audience, legs and feet pointing straight up. The crowd, suddenly still, gawked.

When Mrs. McSneed drew near the audience, she poked her head out from beneath her skirts and cried, "Who has seen the king? Return him to me, I beg you! I need to laugh!"

The audience burst into applause.

It was then that Judy and Punch rushed out and tried to get Mrs. McSneed away.

"Help!" cried Mrs. McSneed. "I'm being stolen! Help!"

Now the crowd began to cheer.

As Judy and Punch struggled to get Mrs. McSneed into the wagon, Judy shouted to Doc, "Tell the crowd it's over! Tell them!"

But Doc was in a state of shock. He could only bleat, "What are you going to do about Zun? He's gone!"

"Tell them the show's over!" Judy cried, working to get her mother back into the wagon. Tears were trickling down her cheeks.

Seeing Doc was not about to do anything, Punch tore away to face the audience, prepared to say the show was over. But the moment he faced the crowd he became tongue-tied. The audience began to hoot. Thrown into confusion, not knowing what else to do, he started to dance the same jig he'd done before. As he did his jumps and jitters, he called, "Alexander! Alexander!"

Alexander poked his snout out from beneath the wagon, then trotted out. Punch grabbed him, pulled him up on his back trotters, and the two began to dance. Alexander grunted.

The audience laughed.

As Alexander and Punch waltzed about, Judy, having stowed her mother away, came back out from the wagon. When she saw what Punch was doing, she stopped. Punch saw her and stopped short, his face red with shame.

The audience, however, began to clap. "More! More!" they called.

Judy, however, announced the show was over. Ne-Nip wasn't even offered.

Thirteen

It was gloomy that evening as the troupe sat around a small fire. The August heat and humidity hardly required warmth, but smoke helped to keep mosquitoes away.

Punch, sitting a bit off from the rest, rubbing Alexander's ears, kept a watch on the others. Judy seemed lost in thought. Horatio, never far from her, kept trying to catch her eye. Twig was fingering pebbles. Zun pulled at his mustache ends, while Doc stroked his beard as if the pulling of it would make him wiser. From time to time Blodger popped his knuckles.

Looking on, Punch was certain that something bad was going to happen. He kept waiting, but in spite of himself he dozed. Then the fire snapped, and as Punch woke he heard Blodger say, "Judy, we any closer to York State?"

"I don't know for sure," Judy admitted.

"About the only thing we *can* count on," Doc said bitterly, "is that Sheriff Oxnard is still after us."

"Ah, Judy, my girl," Twig sighed, "you should have listened to me. All this running away. For what? Poor Da didn't even get himself a decent burying."

Blodger gave a ponderous shake of his head. "It's no good," he said. "At this rate we're going to starve."

"Right," Doc put in, "medically speaking, we either get money, or we're dead."

To which Zun added, "Then we better find a way to get it."

The tense silence that followed was broken only by the click-click of Twig's juggling stones.

Punch stole a glance at Judy. Now and again the flickering light from the fire made her red hair look like it was burning. Unexpectedly, she turned to him. Their eyes met. Her expression contained the same anger he had seen before. But this time, Punch saw something else—a touch of puzzlement—which appeared like a question *he* was supposed to answer.

Before Punch could figure out what that question was, Judy said, "Well, I *have* been thinking about changes." She paused, took a deep breath, then went on. "We're never going to draw people with what we're doing. We need to redo the show."

"Now, Judy, love," Twig drawled. "Let me take the liberty of reminding you that Da knew what he was doing. For years we've gotten through, and sure we'll do it again. You know perfectly well the entire world is down with hard times. An old bird flies no further with new feathers."

"The old show won't work anymore," Judy said.

"Look here, Judy," Blodger said with thickening anger, "if we wanted that kind of talk we could go back and listen to the parson preach. Your job is telling us how we can raise cash. That's all."

"That's exactly what I am doing," Judy said evenly. "Everywhere we go," she went on, "things are bad. There's no money. No jobs anywhere. People are awful low. I think they want something to cheer them up."

Doc frowned. "What kind of medicine you suggesting, then?"

"Be funny," Judy said. "Make people laugh." Her words were met with silent astonishment.

"Funny!" Doc finally sputtered. "How the blazes can you expect serious artists to be *funny?"*

Judy leaned forward. "Do you remember what happened in Bigalow?" she asked.

"A disaster!" Zun said.

"Exactly," Judy agreed. "Nobody was interested in what *we* did. But they *were* interested when Punch performed that silly dance of his. Woke people up. They laughed. Applauded. Well, it happened today—again."

Punch, taken by surprise, could do nothing but stare at Judy.

"Judy," Twig cried, "by all that's sacred, am I hearing you hint that it's Punch here who's going to heave us toward our happiness?"

"It's happened twice," Judy replied stoutly.

Punch's mouth was now agape.

"I've a notion there are some other people here," Blodger growled.

"Everybody has to change," Judy insisted.

"What about Ne-Nip?" Doc demanded. His beard seemed to bristle.

"Useless," Judy said.

"Useless!" Doc squawked. "It's our only money-maker!"

"Not recently," Judy retorted.

"Are we to gather, then," Blodger said with barely suppressed indignation, "that you've been thinking about this for a while?"

"Since Punch did that first dance of his."

"Ain't that something!" Doc spat out. "Her father dies, and all she thinks about is making folks laugh."

Judy, ignoring the remark, continued, "So from now on," she said firmly, "that's what we're going to do. Be funny. Make people laugh."

"May the Lord preserve us!" Twig murmured under his breath.

Saying they needed to confer, the Merry Men went off to talk on their own. Only Judy, Horatio, and Punch remained by the dying fire.

After a while Punch said, "Judy . . ."

"What?"

"I . . . I don't understand."

"There's nothing to understand."

"Did you . . . did you . . . *like* what I did?"

Judy studied the fire. "People liked it," she returned with care. "They laughed."

"But . . . but I don't even know if I can do it again." Punch pleaded. "Not . . . on purpose."

"Punch," Judy said, "there's nothing else." With that remark she got up and went into the wagon. A bewildered Punch watched her go.

After a moment Horatio heaved himself up. "Look here, Punch," he said, "if Judy says you're to be funny, you better do it. That is, if you know what's good for you." Then he, too, went off.

Punch remained alone with Alexander. "Alexander," he whispered. The pig, who had been sleeping, lifted his great head, shook it, and looked around. Punch could make out his red eyes by the reflected glow of the dying fire.

"Do you," Punch asked the pig, "do you think I'm funny?"

The pig blinked sleepily.

"Do you?" Punch insisted.

The pig lowered his head.

"I mean," Punch whispered, "I don't even know what funny *means*. Do you?"

Alexander grunted, closed his eyes, and went back to sleep.

"I think Judy's making a terrible mistake," Punch whispered as he stared into the dying embers. Slowly, he reached into one of the side pockets of his overalls. In the palm of his hand lay the dollar Mr. McSneed had given him four years ago. Though the coin was dirty and nicked, Punch stared at it as if it could provide an answer. When it did not, he carefully replaced the dollar in his pocket, then drifted off to a restless sleep.

Next morning, it was Punch, in search of boots to clean, who discovered that Zun, Doc, and Blodger had all deserted the show.

PART
THREE

One

Stunned, Punch raced to Twig's tent. To his great relief the old man was there, sleeping. But it was still a very frightened Punch who pounded on the wagon door. "Judy!" he shouted. "Judy!"

Judy stuck out her head. "What is it?" she asked sleepily.

"They're gone!" Punch cried. "Blodger, Zun, and Doc. Gone and cleared out. Took off!"

Judy blanched. "You sure?"

"Look for yourself."

When Judy checked and saw that Punch was right, she hastened to wake Twig.

"It's done!" the juggler exclaimed, holding up his trousers with a hand while standing barefoot before the abandoned tents. Then he sat down on the ground, plucked up some pebbles, and began to juggle slowly. "Doom is thy word with evil times a-coming!" he proclaimed. "Our glory days are all behind us!"

When Horatio learned what had happened, he offered to go after the three men.

"But where would you start?" Judy asked helplessly. Suddenly, she turned to Punch. "Did they take Belle?"

"She's out in the field."

Judy allowed herself a sigh of relief, but when Horatio and Punch waited for her to tell them what to do, she only wrapped her arms over her chest and turned away. Even as she did, the wagon door banged open and Mrs. McSneed burst out, dived off the wagon, did three flips, then landed on her hands. "The Queen of Tipperary has arrived!" she announced. "Where is the laughter?"

All that morning they waited in hopes the three men would return. By afternoon, when they hadn't, Twig announced he'd go to town. "If they're there," he said, "I'll haul them back."

Judy looked into his eyes. "Please, Twig," she implored, "don't you go leaving, too."

Giving her no reply other than a reproachful look, the old man left. Punch watched him go, unable to keep from wondering if he would return. Then he went to Horatio. "I don't think we have much food," Punch informed him.

"There's always your pig," Horatio said.

Shocked, Punch stepped back.

Horatio laughed. "I'll see what I can do. Think I saw a farm not too far back." Telling Judy he was going in search of something to eat, he, too, set out.

After making sure that Alexander was safe, Punch took a place where he could keep and eye on Judy. Sometimes she was in the wagon with Mrs. McSneed. At other times, she wandered restlessly abut the camp. Not once did she approach Punch. Convinced she was avoiding him, it added to his feeling that he was the cause of what had happened. How he wished he had never done that dance!

Horatio returned, chicken in hand.

"Where'd you get that?" Punch asked with admiration.

"Borrowed it from that farm over the hill," Horatio replied with a wink. "Get some water."

Punch hurried to fetch it. When he returned, Twig had also come back.

"If the lads went through town," he was informing Judy, "they left no trace. Gone, sure as youth. But I'll tell you who was there."

"Who?" Judy asked.

"Sheriff Oxnard."

Horatio gasped.

"Spied the ugly myself," Twig went on. "Not that he saw me. Well, here's praying those loutish lads of ours didn't mark us out, or we're likely to have unwanted company for dinner."

"Do you have any notion how far we are from the York border?" Judy asked.

"I was in such a hurry to bring my news, I forgot to ask."

It did not matter. By common consent, they packed up quickly and set off, not pausing to eat.

Horatio guided Belle. Punch, with Alexander at his side, kept glancing back over his shoulder, expecting to see the sheriff thundering down upon them.

"If you're asking my opinion," Twig told Judy as they tramped along side by side, "though you've paid me no mind since Da died, it's this: Head for the nearest city. That should be Albany. We'll recruit replacements and carry on as before."

"No," Judy said doggedly.

"For blessed sake, Judy! After all our grief, do you still intend to fumble forward with being funny?"

"Yes."

"And with that one?" Twig said, gesturing contemptuously toward Punch.

"He's all we have."

"Judy, darling, look here. I'm not likely to sneak off the way them turncoats have done. I'm too loyal to you, your ma, and the memory of Da. But by all that's left of life in me, what you find funny in that sorry excuse of a boy passes my mortal understanding."

"If you'd just help him, Twig," Judy pleaded, "it could work."

"Judy," the juggler replied, "let me tell you something my own ma told me. 'Twiglet,' she says, and she preparing to meet her God, 'pouring water into a leaky soul is only wetting worms beneath the sod.' "

Judy made no reply.

At the end of their frantic march they made camp at an abandoned farm where weeds were high and fences down. The barn roof had collapsed while the farmhouse—behind which they set themselves so as to keep hidden from the road—was gutted and fringed with soot. It suited them well.

Punch had lit a fire and was roasting old potatoes that Twig had found. He was also boiling a couple of cups of corn kernels which Horatio had scavenged from a crib. "All right then, gal," Twig was saying to Judy, "what kind of being funny would you like?"

"Whatever makes people laugh," she replied.

"Won't do," Twig warned. "Funny isn't so simple. Look here," he said, holding up his hands and ticking off fingers. "There's sly humor, word jokes and the like, which take clever speaking. But you need a quick crowd to grasp it, which we don't usually get. On the other end there's gross humor, which takes no deep thought at all, like falling off a chair when the audience

least expects it. That's cheap, low stuff, which no serious artist—like us—should do this side of desperation.

"Then there's what's called satire, which is a high-toned kind of mockery. But America has a bad mix of thick skulls and thin skins, so we'd best avoid all that. Then there's tall tales, short quips, and braggart speeches like the politicians do, save they don't even notice. 'Course, there's rude remarks, funny getups, nasty put-downs, and a whole lot besides. So, you see, you have to decide which you want."

"Whatever Punch does best," Judy said.

"Judy," Twig exclaimed with exasperation, "I'm telling you, the boy don't know jokes from jades. Here, I'll show you."

He fetched an old barrel and set it up on one end. "Punch!" he cried. "Come over here."

"Now?" Punch said, becoming instantly alarmed.

Twig nodded. "You heard Judy say we're putting a

new shine on the show, and you're the first rub. So up you go. On that." He pointed to the barrel.

Punch made a mute appeal to Judy.

"Do what he says," she said.

Punch limped over to the barrel. Horatio took his place by the fire.

"All right, my boyo," Twig said, laying a hand on Punch's shoulder, "what we want is a hint as to your hidden hilarity."

With great reluctance, Punch climbed atop the wobbly barrel and stood there in complete misery.

Twig took a place before him. "Now then," he began, "let's cast about for some of your giggle."

Punch, looking everywhere but at those around him, squirmed. "I . . . don't feel funny," he squeaked.

Horatio peered around with a grin.

"Well now," Twig prompted, "how about doing the likes of what you did the other day? That famous dance of yours."

"Dance?" Punch replied with shame.

"Starting at the low end of normal," Twig said.

Tears building, Punch appealed to Judy once again, but all she said was, "Try, Punch."

Deciding he should at least attempt to please Judy, Punch struggled to recall what he'd done. At last, though deeply embarrassed by the staring eyes, he lifted his arms and started to wave them about loosely. But hardly did he begin than he dropped them. The humiliation was too great.

"Judy . . ." Punch beseeched and, forgetting he was standing on a barrel, took a step forward and tumbled atop Twig.

"Get off me! You bloody fool!" Twig cried.

Punch leaped up and fled.

Horatio found him hiding beneath the corncrib. On hands and knees, he peered at Punch, who had rolled himself up into a tight ball. "Judy's waiting for you," he called.

"I can't do it," Punch whimpered.

"You did it before."

"It was an accident!"

With a sudden snatch, Horatio caught hold of Punch's arm and dragged him from his place like a wounded rabbit.

"I can't! I can't!" Punch screamed, squirming desperately to get away.

Horatio shook Punch hard. "Do what she tells you to do, understand?"

"I don't know how to be funny," Punch wailed. "I don't!"

Horatio set a fist before Punch's nose. "Look here," he said in a voice as hard as nails. "She's depending on you. If you fail, do you know what I'm going to do?"

Punch shook his head.

"I'm going to thrash you."

Punch wilted.

"All right then," Horatio said, "come along and be funny."

Once more Punch was upon the barrel. Twig stood before him while Horatio, on guard, leaned against the wagon, holding up a fist as warning. A grim Judy, sitting on the wagon backboard, watched.

"All right, lad," Twig pressed, "we're still waiting on that funny dance of yours."

With a painful shyness that numbed his limbs and made it hard to breathe, Punch sniffled, gulped, wiped his nose, smeared tears off with the back of his hand, and offered up one more beseeching glance toward Judy.

All she said was, "Try."

Resigned, Punch turned back to Twig. The old man leaned out of his plaid coat and cried, "Here we go!" and began to clap his hands to set a beat.

Punch took a few clumsy steps.

"There you are!" Twig cried by way of encouragement. "But a tad more of the old enthusiastic!" And he increased the tempo of his clapping. Punch jigged and jogged some more.

"Hands!" Twig cried. "Hands!"

Punch lifted his arms—they felt like lead pipes—and began to wave his fingers about in floppy fashion.

"Roll your eyes!" Twig shouted. "That always gets them!"

Punch forced himself to do it.

"Better!" Twig cried. "Better! Fingers farther out. Keep them loose. That's it! You're getting it. There you are! Now, more with your arms. Like they weren't part of you. And those eyes. They're all over the place but front. Not so miserable, boy! Be happy! Stifle them tears! You're young and life's a pack of pleasure and a smile says it's so! Enjoy yourself! Move them legs! Faster! Faster!"

That time the whole barrel collapsed.

As Punch lay on the ground, exhausted, he heard Twig cry, "By God, Judy, you might be right. Needs work, but there's laughter lurking in the loathsome lad!"

Two

A slender born of moon hung in the hot and heavy darkness. Alexander, stretched by Punch's side, occasionally opened his eyes, flitted them in the boy's direction, and grunted, only to fall asleep again.

"What are we going to do?" an exhausted Punch asked the pig. "I know it's for Judy, but if they make me do those things in front of other people, I'll die. I just know I will."

Alexander made no response.

With a sigh Punch got up and went over to the wagon. Judy was sitting on the backboard, her head resting on Horatio's shoulder, while he had his arm around her waist. The two were watching Mrs. McSneed by the light of the lamp. She was doing countless cartwheels.

Punch took in the sight, then approached timidly. "Judy," he called softly.

Judy looked around. Horatio sprang up as though to protect her.

"I have to speak to you," Punch whispered.

Judy touched Horatio gently. "Go," she said. As Horatio walked off, he gave Punch a menacing look. For a moment Judy and Punch watched Mrs. McSneed. She was now standing on one leg while her other leg

curled around and touched the top of her head. All the while she was staring into the darkness.

"Do you see the way she is now?" Judy said. "Right in the middle of her act, she'll stand still like that. I do wonder what she's seeing. But when I call her . . . Mama! Mama!"

For a fleeting moment Mrs. McSneed's face became soft.

"You see," Judy said sadly, "sometimes I think she *does* hear me. But then, nothing. Oh, Punch, maybe she's getting better." The sweetness of Judy's tone— so rare those days—fairly melted Punch. But then her voice took on the more familiar hard edge when she said, "What did you want to talk to me about?"

"It's this being . . . funny," Punch began. "I hate it. Do . . . do I have to do it?"

Judy studied him for a long time. "Look here, Punch," she finally said, "you know as well as I do the show's all but dead. Do you have any other ideas about what we could do to keep it going?"

Punch shook his head.

"I'm going to try something different, too," she said. "Even Horatio's looking for an act. And Twig says he's getting a whole new idea. Something fine. He'll tell us soon. But, Punch . . ."

"What?"

"You're the natural fool."

"I am?"

"And a good one."

"Judy?"

"What?"

"What if I'm not . . . fool enough?"

At first Judy said nothing. Mrs. McSneed, meanwhile, began doing back flips. Then Judy said, "We'll have to break up."

Punch examined his toes. "But . . . then . . . what would happen to . . . me?" He looked up. By the flickering lamplight he saw the now-familiar flash of anger in Judy's eyes. Suddenly, he cried, "Why are you so angry with me?"

Judy turned away.

"Was it something I did?" he begged.

Judy shook her head.

"Can't you tell me? *Please?*"

"The York border can't be that far off," Judy replied coldly. "Go on to sleep now. Go on."

Punch limped way. As he went he could hear Mrs. McSneed cry, "Where's the king who made me laugh? When will he return?"

Three

Early the next morning they started off again. But they seemed to have entered upon a blasted place. Everywhere they looked, disaster appeared to have crushed the land. Houses were abandoned. Fields lay untilled. The road itself was rutted and full of holes, some the size of kettles. And as the day wore on, an awful heat crushed them all. Their steps dragged. Sweat dripped. Belle, head drooping, legs lagging, slowed her pace more and more. Even Alexander, trotting under the wagon for shade, had a lolling tongue.

By midafternoon they reached a crossroad with a sign:

FARKTWIST 5½ Miles
YORK STATE LINE 6 Miles

"Almost there!" Twig said with relief. And so they pushed on.

While Horatio and Judy stayed up front with Belle, Punch went along with Twig.

"The whole thing to being funny, my boy," the juggler explained, "is to show folks you got the love of life. You can't throw a pity party for yourself in front

of an audience. On the other hand, faked grins won't do it either. People see through all of that. So you'll need to work on your smile and wink till they get to looking real. And while you're at it, if you could get those eyes of your looking straight, it would do wonders. It's all a way of hinting you don't mind being alive. That's a trick folks will buy.

"You see, Punch," Twig continued, "being funny isn't like magic, with people enjoying being fooled. Nor like your ropewalker either, where your audience likes the skill of the thing. No, the whole twist to being funny is to make your audience feel safe in their souls. For once, someone else is fool, not them. Mind, you have a major advantage there, Punch, 'cause you're a natural-born idiot if ever there was one.

"Now for myself," Twig went on, "I've been racking my brains for a comic song or two for a new opening. Your audience likes a clever song with a hint of naughty to start things off. Makes them feel bold when they're not.

"As for Horatio—between you and me—the lad's shaded to the dull side of life, and maybe that's why Judy sparks to him, opposites attracting, you know. So what I'm thinking, Punch, is, it's magic for him.

"As for Judy, well, I've begun to lay out the grandest scheme of all—in my head. I'll announce it soon. Oh, it's a beaut, my boy. A beaut!

"But it's you," he continued, "that's supposed to be our flame and fame, lad. So, even as we're walking, let's put this hellish heat out of mind. No mind to Mrs. McSneed's madness. Banish the fear that our show is teetering on the fringe of finality or that maybe that ugly sheriff is set on another ambush. Push all that stuff aside. What I want from you is—smiles."

"Right now?"

"I'll be straight with you, lad. Your smiles are uncommon rare. You need to practice. Here. Look around at me."

The wagon had stopped. Punch wondered what the matter was.

"Never mind that," Twig insisted as he pulled Punch about. "Set your eyes on me. Both together, lad. There, you're getting close. Now, give us some cock-locky like the lords of England have."

Punch grimaced.

"Won't do, lad. The world gives coin only to the cheerful beggar. Try again."

Punch squeezed out another grin.

"Lad, you're looking like the man who's swallowed a slug when he'd been offered a sweet.

"Here now, think on this. Imagine you're in love with the loveliest gal in the whole world, the very image of an angel. Now, I know it won't happen to a misbegotten mug like you, but this lady—your heart's deepest desire—finally says she's mad in love with you. So, what do you do, you smile! Not tears, you fool!" Twig roared. *"Smiles!"*

Judy rushed up to them. "Something's the matter with Belle!"

Belle stood between the wagon shafts, her head bent so low her nose was near touching the ground.

"She won't move," Judy said, wiping away the hair that was sticking to her sweaty face. "We can't go any further."

Four

Horatio examined Belle carefully. "She's sick with the heat," he finally announced. "She needs water."

Twig looked about. "There's a farm over there," he said, pointing to a house perched on a hill, a quarter of a mile away. "Punch, go borrow some wet."

Bucket in hand, Punch walked up the weed-filled path to the house. It was a two-story wooden structure with most of its shingles missing, almost all of its windows punched out, and at least one roof hole that Punch could see. In the front yard was a pump, red with rust.

He stepped onto the porch. Many of the boards were rotten. The floor sagged and squeaked. When he touched one of the pillars that supported the porch roof, it wobbled.

Though the front door hung on just one hinge, Punch knocked. No one answered. Cautiously, he walked into a large kitchen. Tattered remains of curtains hung on windows. A braided rug, mouse-chewed, lay on the floor. In the middle of the room were a table and chairs. Dishes, most broken, along with bent forks and knives, were strewn about.

Punch took it all in, wondering what it would be like

to live in such a grand place. Then, remembering why he'd come, he hurried to the pump. After some time it produced a yellowish trickle of water. Punch carried the bucket back to Belle, who drank greedily.

"She needs to rest," Horatio advised.

Judy turned to Punch. "What's up there?"

"Abandoned farm," Punch said. "People left most everything."

"Judy, love," Twig cautioned, "that state line is blessed close. Once across we can rest for days."

Judy looked to Horatio.

"Belle can't go anymore," Horatio insisted.

"Being cooped up all the time can't do Mama any good," Judy said. "Stopping in a real house might even help. And resting here will give us time to put the new show together."

"Judy . . ." Twig cautioned.

"No," she said, "we'll stay."

Judy led her mother into a first-floor room, taking one for herself next door. Twig found himself a place on the second floor. Horatio strolled through the house, trying windows, checking doors. "This could be fixed," he kept saying, testing one thing or another. "Nothing we couldn't set right."

Punch found a small room on the top floor. It was completely bare, with but one small glass window intact. He rubbed away its film of dirt, then pressed his face against the cool glass, marveling that he was inside when all the world was out. For a moment he thought of the many places he had lived. Suddenly, as though a hidden window opened, he recalled one particular house. The memory was vague and very old. There was a family. And war. And an explosion. The vision vanished, leaving him with only a limp.

With sweat on his brow and a quickened pulse, Punch recollected where he was. He looked below. In the barnyard Alexander was gazing up. Hurriedly, Punch made his way down.

"I've been searching all over for you," Judy said when she found Punch in the barn. He was sprawled on a pile of old hay. Alexander lay nearby.

"Don't you want a room in the house?" she asked.

"Alexander wouldn't go up the steps," Punch explained. Then, suddenly realizing that Judy seemed sadder than usual, he said, "Is Mrs. McSneed all right?"

"She's happy just sitting in her room looking out a window. I think being in a house has already calmed her." Judy wandered about, gazing at the rafters, watching barn swallows.

Punch decided she was upset. "Anything the matter?" he asked, sitting up.

Without looking at him, Judy said, "Horatio says there's nothing the matter with this place. Not really. With work it could all be fixed up. He's already put the front door back on its proper hinges." She looked around at Punch. "Why do you think the people left?"

"Don't know."

"Perhaps," Judy said, her voice turning dreamy, "they left it for us." She stood there, gazing vacantly out the barn door. Punch watched her intently.

"Punch . . ." Judy said at last.

"What?"

"Horatio and I are going to walk down the road a piece. To that town. Farktwist."

"Want me to watch your ma?"

"Would you? We won't be gone long. Twig found some tools. He's putting his idea together."

"What idea?"

"For the new show. Says it's something for you and me. Won't tell what until it's done."

"For *both* of us?" Punch asked, pleased but not sure he should show it.

"We'll have to see," Judy said. Suddenly, she came to where he was sitting, bent over, and kissed Punch on his cheek. Then she turned and fled out of the barn.

For a long time Punch stayed still, not wanting to do anything that would cause him to lose the sweet sensation that lingered on his cheek. But even as the kiss faded, the realization of what Judy had done grew.

"Alexander!" he cried with growing excitement. "Alexander!"

The pig jumped up, trotted over from the far side of the barn, and looked up at him.

"Did you see what Judy did?" Punch asked, his voice trembling with the thrill. "Did you?"

Alexander gazed up without comprehension.

"She doesn't hate me!" Punch whispered, his heart fluttering like a delirious butterfly. *"Judy doesn't hate me!"*

Now Punch became so excited he leaped up and began to run in place, his feet tattooing the old barn floor. He kicked up his heels. He slapped his knees. With a yelp of raucous rapture, he shouted, "Judy doesn't hate Punch! Judy doesn't hate Punch!"

And then Punch flung out his arms as wide as possible, spread his fingers taut, threw back his head, laughed, and right then and right there danced to the sweetest music that ever piped in human heart!

Five

Mrs. McSneed sat in a chair staring at Punch. Her face, perfectly bland, revealed neither feelings nor thoughts.

"*Punch*," Punch said, tapping himself on the chest. "My name is *Punch*."

Mrs. McSneed's face appeared to soften. For a moment Punch thought she even recognized him. But then she said, "Who are you?"

"I just said—Punch."

"Do I know you—Punch?"

"Sure do. Mr. McSneed found me years ago. Nobody but him wanted me to stay. I've been with the troupe ever since."

"I am the Queen of Tipperary."

"No, you're not," Punch replied, his voice kindly. "You're Mrs. McSneed."

"McSneed?"

"Sure. Everyone knows that. And Mrs. McSneed, I want to tell you how fine your Judy is."

"Who is . . . Judy?"

"Judy's your daughter. I think a whole lot about her."

Mrs. McSneed's brow furrowed. Then she stood up,

and spun five times on one toe, after which she did the same on her head.

Punch, not paying much mind to what she was doing, went on. "Fact is, I love Judy. And, you know, someday I'm going to marry her. Of course, when I do, I'll take care of you, too. You've got my promise on that."

Mrs. McSneed, who was now standing on one hand, asked, "Will the king return?"

"Da, you mean? Afraid not."

Mrs. McSneed hopped about the room on her hands. "Why?" she asked.

"Well, see, he died."

"How sad."

Twig poked his head around the door. "Sssst!" he called to Punch. "Let her be and come on out. I've got something to show you."

"Be right back," Punch said to Mrs. McSneed. "That okay?"

Gracefully untying the knot into which she had tied herself, Mrs. McSneed returned to her chair. Then, just as Punch was about to go out the door, she called, "Punch!"

"That's me."

"You said . . . I know you."

"That's right. *Punch.*"

"I see," Mrs. McSneed said. Folding her hands in her lap, she became thoughtful.

Six

"Now, what do you think of this?" Twig said when Punch joined him outside. The old man was holding up two sticks, each three feet long. At one end they were attached by whipcord to form a handle.

"What is it?" Punch wondered.

Instead of answering, Twig lifted the sticks with one hand and brought them down hard onto the palm of his other hand. There was a loud crack, so loud and unexpected that Punch jumped.

"Pretty fine, isn't it?" Twig said, giving his hand another crack.

"Doesn't that hurt?" Punch had to ask.

"That's it exactly," Twig replied, a sly grin upon his face. "It don't hurt at all. It's a slap-stick. Go on, hold out your hand. Do it."

Punch held out his hand.

Soon as he did, Twig brought his slap-stick around and tried to strike Punch's palm. But at the last moment Punch jerked back.

"No, no," Twig cried, "you're not understanding. Look here. It won't do harm. The sound you're hearing is just one stick slapping the other, *not* my hand. That's why it's called a slap-stick. Now go on, put out your hand again."

Cautiously, Punch thrust his hand forward. Before he could draw it away, Twig brought down the slap-stick and hit the hand with a loud crack. "That hurt?" he asked.

"Nothing but a tingle," Punch admitted.

"That's it," Twig cried, "that's it exactly. No pain to it at all. It only *looks* like it hurts. Which is the joke. See this here?" He pointed to a small piece of wood lodged between the long pieces right before the handle. "That bit of wood there is the whole secret to slap-sticks. Long as it stays there, no one gets hurt."

"But what are you going to do with the thing?" Punch wanted to know.

"Punch, it's the idea of my life," Twig proclaimed. "The acme of my achievements. What we're going to do is a live—*live*—Punch and Judy show!"

"I don't understand."

"Well now, folks know Punch and Judy as a puppet show," Twig went on, getting more and more excited. "They're a twosome, you see, married, and they're always getting into funny scrapes and scuffles. Of course, we're going to do it *live*, thereby establishing the only live Punch and Judy show in the entire universe. It's your own true names, too, Punch and Judy, so it's a natural!"

Punch, beginning to get the idea, smiled.

"Punch," Twig said with a swelling pride, "you're going to be the sensation of the nation! Soon as Judy gets back from town, I'll inform her. I'm telling you, she'll be in love with the notion, too!"

For the rest of the day Twig and Punch rehearsed. Punch learned routines, memorized lines, worked through all the bits of action. And the more they practice, the more excited Twig became.

"I'll admit to it," the juggler said, taking a moment to adjust the slap-stick wedge, "Judy was right. You've got the gift. Now, Punch, I'll ask you, do you think McSneed knew it when he took you in all those years ago? Do you?"

"Don't know," Punch said.

"I don't doubt it for a moment," Twig gushed on. "And to think I never saw your talent."

Punch beamed.

By the time Punch finished rehearsing with Twig— with occasional checks on Mrs. McSneed—he was exhausted. Even so, there was an excitement running through him that had him giggling while he cleaned the oven and gathered wood. As he swept the kitchen, he couldn't wait for Judy and Horatio to get back.

The two returned around twilight. And it was a somber couple who came through the front door.

The instant they came in, Twig sprang up and cried, "Judy, my love, I've got the whole new show worked to perfection!"

Judy and Horatio exchanged looks. Horatio gave a slight shake of his head. Punch saw it. Instantly, he sensed that something important had happened.

"Look here, Judy," Twig rushed on, slapping a scrap of paper on which he had been designing a new hand-

bill. 'Joe McSneed and His Merry Men' is going to become the boom of the blessed world."

Judy, as though not hearing, turned to Punch and asked, "How's Mama?"

"Sleeping," Punch answered, trying to grasp what had occurred.

"As you can see here," Twig rushed on, not sensing anything amiss, "I'll be leading off with a funny song I've recalled. Might even juggle a bit, seeing as how the old bits don't fail to tickle the tykes. Then, after that, we'll have Horatio do a turn of magic. It's stuff Doc taught me. Don't worry none, lad. We'll work you easy. Disappearing cards and all those turvy bits.

"After that, we'll give the stage over to Punch here, who'll do his famous jig. That'll hasten the house toward hilarity. Judy, my love, you were right. The lad lifts a load of talent."

"Now, Judy," Twig continued, getting more and

more excited, "what comes next is the grandest thing of all. The idea of my lifetime. Why, if I'd come up with this in times gone by, I'd have been a rich man by now. You're going to swear I'm a blooming genius, and indeed I'm inclined to the truth of that myself.

"See this?" Twig cried, brandishing the slap-stick. "I've been working with Punch here on how it's used, going over the business the entire afternoon. All we need do is practice with you. Then we'll try it out.

"What we're doing—listen sharp now—is a *live* Punch and Judy show! Can't you see it, Judy? *A live Punch and Judy show!* Why, we'll be soaring to the top of the bills. No saying where it'll carry us. How big is this here Farktwist?" he demanded. "Big enough for a show?"

Judy looked to Horatio. Then, lamely, she said, "Maybe two hundred."

"No harm in starting small," Twig said. "Smooth the odd edge. But quick as the hungry flea hops, we'll be hurtling on to greater heights. To Albany! To Boston, New York, and London! Then, best of all, back to Dublin! Now what do you say to that? Ain't I the fairest genius to grace this earth?"

Punch caught Judy glancing at Horatio again. That time Horatio gave a short nod. Punch, certain something awful was about to happen, hardly dared to breathe.

Judy turned back to Twig. "Twig, I have to tell you—and Punch—something important." Her voice trembled.

Twig looked at Judy—then at Horatio—then back to Judy again. "Important?" the old man sputtered with indignation. "What's more important than what I've been telling you?"

"Twig," Judy said, "in town, just now, Horatio and I . . . got married."

The moment Punch heard the words, he felt as if his heart stopped beating. Then a roaring came into his head, and his throat tightened like a fist. But all he could do was fix disbelieving eyes on Judy.

As for Twig, he stared at Judy stupidly. *"Married?"* he croaked. "Just now? This afternoon? While you were gone off?" His voice kept going up, ending in a mouselike squeak.

Judy, nodding, gave a nervous smile.

"The . . . the . . . *two* of you?" Twig asked, pointing first to Judy and then to Horatio.

"Yes," Judy said with a blush. "At the courthouse."

Punch tried to swallow. He could not. He felt sick. He was suffocating. He was certain he was dying.

"But . . . but . . ." Twig managed. "That's all to the fine and good, but after all, well, it don't stop the clock, does it? Bravo to the bride, glory to the groom, and all the cheerful cant of cuteness. But what I'm meaning to say, Judy, married or no, we'll be needing to get on with the new show—"

"Twig," Horatio interrupted, "I don't know what my plans are yet."

"Who the devil cares what *your* plans are, you misbegotten imitation of a wooden stick!" Twig roared with indignation. His nose red, his eyes glazed with tears, Twig turned back to Judy with supplicating hands. "Judy, love," he said in tattered tones, "this new show I've been working on, it's all you asked for. And more. The climaxing finish to a glorious life of performing art. My chance. The greatest hope I've ever hoped and—"

It was then that Punch, who had been trying to contain the tumultuous emotions he felt, could hold himself

116

back no more. "Liar!" he suddenly screamed at Judy, his face twisting with a fury he had never allowed himself to feel before. "Cheat! Fake! I hate you!"

Then, wanting to do nothing but run to the end of the world and leap off, he rushed to the door and yanked it open. There, standing on the threshold, was Sheriff Oxnard.

Seven

Grinning with glee, rocking back on his heels with pleasure, Sheriff Oxnard gazed at each person in the room.

"Now that was some chase, wasn't it?" he drawled, stepping boldly into the house. "Moving from town to town as if you didn't know where you were going. But you were heading for York State, weren't you? That was clear enough. So when I saw the two of you"—he nodded toward Judy and Horatio—"holding hands at

Farktwist like Adam and Eve out for a noontime stroll in Eden, it was easy enough to follow you here. But now—you're all under arrest."

Judy, Horatio, and Twig were all too stunned to say a word. As for Punch, he was so frightened he could only push himself into a far corner and stand there trembling.

The sheriff, with a calculated casualness that measured his pleasure, pulled out a sheaf of papers. "Got me a bunch of warrants for each of you," he informed them. "Nobody need feel left out. Nobody. Why," he said, "I've got a public-nuisance charge. A resisting-lawful-arrest charge. A fleeing-the-place-of-a-crime charge. Selling-false-medicine charge. Attacking-a-law-officer-in-the-performance-of-his-duty charge. Under-age-minors charge. Even a dangerous-and-violent-pig charge. Each offense dutifully witnessed and sworn by Parson Brutus Cuthwhip, esquire. You need anything more?"

They were still too numb to speak.

"Now," the sheriff continued, "I'm supposed to read these off to you, and I will, too, because it's pleasant for me to hear."

Licking his thumb with an excess of spit, Oxnard peeled off the top paper. "We'll start with this one. For a—Phinias Blodger. That you?" he demanded of Twig.

"Not at all," Twig said, drawing himself up a little straighter. "Mr. Blodger has gone."

"What do you mean, *gone?*"

"He left the troupe some time ago," Judy explained.

"And so did Mr. Pudlow and Mr. Zunbadden," Horatio chimed in quickly. "We don't know where. And we aren't selling anything that you might call medicine either. That was Dr. Pudlow's product."

Sheriff Oxnard frowned and hastily thumbed through more of his papers, scattering useless warrants on the floor until he held up another sheet. "Judy McSneed," he said. "That's you, I suppose."

Judy shook her head. "No more."

"What's that supposed to mean?" Oxnard growled suspiciously.

"I've changed my name. I'm married now."

"Married? To whom?"

"Me," Horatio said, boldly putting his arm about Judy's waist.

"When?"

"Just today. In Farktwist. That's when you must have seen us."

Sheriff Oxnard's eyes narrowed to slits. "Parson Cuthwhip know about this?"

"Don't care if he does," Horatio replied. "I'm of age."

"Well, your father didn't swear out a warrant for you anyway," the sheriff said as he tossed away the warrant. "In fact, he gave a sermon proving you were already damned, and disowned you."

He extracted another paper. " 'Twiger' it says here."

"No one here by the name of *Twiger*," the old juggler proclaimed loftily. "The name is Mr. Patrick Brennen Matthew Twiglet, the *third*."

Oxnard frowned and threw away another sheet. There were two papers left. He studied the first, then looked up with a bright eye.

" 'Punch,' " he announced. "What about an orphan boy called Punch, wanted for being underage? That you?" He pointed a blunt, dirty finger at Punch.

Punch pressed himself further into the corner.

"Is it?" the sheriff demanded.

"Yes, sir . . ." Punch whispered.

"I don't suppose that since this warrant was drawn, you've gone and got yourself married, now have you?"

"No, sir . . ."

"Or changed your name to something more normal than Punch?"

"No, sir . . ."

"Gotten older than twelve?"

"No, sir . . ."

"Found anyone who wants to be your parent?"

Punch shook his head.

"Delighted to confirm it. Then you're still an unmarried, incompetent, homeless orphan." He held up the paper. "Consider yourself under the court's protection."

Punch looked about wildly.

Sheriff Oxnard, paying no mind, studied the last of his papers. "Oh, yes. The pig. I think I saw a black-and-white pig out front. He's the mad beast who bit the parson, isn't he? He'll have to be destroyed. My office claims the meat.

"As for the rest, I'll admit, I can't touch you. But as for you—" He beckoned to Punch. "Come along."

Suddenly Twig thrust himself forward to prevent Punch from moving. "Begging your pardon, sir," he called. Sheriff Oxnard looked about.

"Not wishing," Twig said, "to interfere with the rightfulness of your high-minded legal affairs, but I'd like to say that we were about to pass on over the state line and we could promise we'd never—"

"Don't waste your words," the sheriff cut in. "Parson Cuthwhip swore these warrants, and I've spent a lot of time tracking you down. The least I can do is bring back something. Come along, boy. We need to snare that pig."

Deeply frightened, but not knowing what else to do, Punch began to inch forward. But Twig grabbed an arm and held him.

"Now, sir," Twig said to the sheriff, "you didn't get my meaning. I assure you, this theatrical company is an entirely different enterprise from what it was. Comedy is all we do now. Nothing but laughter."

"Laughter?" the sheriff said with a sneer. "You?"

"Absolutely," Twig insisted. "And if you please, sir, this boy, Punch, is the absolute core of all our comedy."

Oxnard eyed Punch doubtfully.

"A positive genius for the tickle bone," Twig insisted, clutching Punch even tighter. "He's to laughter as blindness is to justice."

"He looks miserable as all get-out," the sheriff said.

"I assure you, sir, we can't exist without him."

"I'm not interested—"

"You doubt me," Twig cried with even greater urgency as he clung to Punch. "But, sir, by heaven and hell and all that squats between, why, this boy could make . . . even *you* laugh!"

The sheriff scrutinized Punch with such a palpable mix of contempt and disbelief that the boy had to close his eyes. Then he snorted and said, "I make it a point never to laugh."

"To be sure, sir," Twig exclaimed, "anyone could see that for themselves! But I'm so altogether certain that this dear boy—and the rest of us—can make even you laugh, why, I'll be offering you a rare bargain."

"What sort of a bargain?" the sheriff asked suspiciously.

"You give us leave to perform for you, say, tomorrow noon. And mind, if we manage to make you laugh, why, you'll let him go free. Now, if he don't make you laugh, why, you can take him . . . and"—Twig looked wildly around the room in search of something to make his bargain irresistible. "Right!" he cried. "If we don't make you laugh," he said, "not only can you take the lad—you can take the rest of us as well!"

"I'll agree to no such thing!" Judy cried.

"Don't listen to her," Twig shouted. "I'm offering an honest deal."

The sheriff looked about the room with a smirk. "Are you saying that if I don't laugh, you'll all *volunteer* to come back to New Moosup?"

"Exactly," Twig said. "But if you *do* laugh, you let Punch go."

"No!" Judy said emphatically.

"Come along, boy," the sheriff cried.

"Judy!" Twig cried, clinging to Punch. "Have mercy on the boy!"

Judy stood and looked at Punch. She looked at Horatio. She looked at Twig and she looked at Sheriff Oxnard. But most of all she gazed at Punch. As she did, a tear slid down the boy's cheek. At that Judy bowed her head and whispered, "All right."

A cruel smile spread across the sheriff's face. "Twiger, you've got yourself a deal," he said. "I'll be back tomorrow noon. And you all might as well know it now: The *last* thing I intend to do is laugh."

Eight

Punch sat on the floor, hugging his knees. His head was down so no one could see his face. Between sobs he cried, "I won't do it! I won't!"

"See here, lad," Twig cried, looking to Judy and Horatio for support. "I only made the deal for you."

"You did it for yourself!" Punch cried. His whole body was shaking.

"By all the saints, past, present, and yet to come!" Twig implored, hand to heart. "I'm speaking holy truth. Being blessed with an uncanny insight into people, I can assure you that despite the sheriff's ugly exterior, he's weak as wet within. Lad, I'm here to say he'll laugh and dance with heels on high. Take my promise for it! And mind if he doesn't, he takes the rest of us, too. I believe in you that much!"

"Go away!" Punch cried.

"Talk to him," Twig said, appealing to Judy. "Make him understand that all we need do is one show and we'll be free."

Judy knelt down. "Punch . . ."

Sniffling, Punch shook his head.

"Listen to me . . ."

"No!"

"But he'll take you away," Judy cried.

"I don't care!"

Judy looked over to Horatio, but her new husband merely shrugged. Then she turned back to Punch and said, "All right. Punch and I will have to talk. The two of you leave."

Twig quickly, Horatio reluctantly, left the room. As for Punch, he was too miserable to care what Judy was going to say. So he stayed where he was, burrowing into himself even more.

Judy remained silent until Punch finally looked up, his face grief-stricken and tear-stained. "I'm going to jail," he croaked.

"Do as Twig says," Judy returned, "and you won't."

Punch shook his head wildly.

"You're being stubborn," Judy said.

Suppressing his sobs, Punch whispered, "Why did you do it?"

"Do what?"

"Get married."

Judy put her hands on her hips. "Is *that* what's ailing you?"

Between rising sobs Punch managed a tiny nod.

Judy let out a sigh, flicked the hair from around her neck, then reached to put a hand on Punch's shoulder. He wanted to pull away, but didn't. He loved the feel of her touch.

"Horatio is good, Punch," Judy said. "And he loves me. As I love him. There wasn't time to tell you, but in town, we learned we can stay here in the house. The people who owned it went off to the Dakotas in search of gold. So if we want the house, it's ours. Then we can decide what we want to do. A real choice.''

Punch shook his head. "Ever since Da died, you've been angry at me!" he wailed. "As if it were my fault!"

Judy's face paled. She went to stare out a window. Punch, wiping away his tears, watched her carefully.

At last Judy turned back to him. "Punch," she said, "remember your asking what it was that Da said to me just before he died? Do you?"

"Yes . . ."

"I wasn't going to tell you. Not until you came of age. Well, I'm going to tell you now. You need to know."

Forgetting his misery, Punch gazed at Judy. She seemed very beautiful to him.

"On the day Da knew he was dying," Judy continued, "he called me to him. You knew that."

Punch nodded.

"Punch . . . he needed . . . to tell me what he wanted

done with the show. And he made me swear I'd do just as he said. So of course I did swear. Then, Punch, he told me . . ." Judy, unable to control her emotions, stopped speaking.

"Told you *what?*" Punch coaxed.

Judy took a breath and went on haltingly. "He told me *I* was to be the boss of the show—not Mama—and keep it together. Yes, I was . . . to keep it together, until . . ." Once again she paused, gathering strength to go on. "Keep it together until . . . you reached your age, then . . . then I was to share it equal—half and half—with . . . you."

Punch stared at her in total disbelief. *"Me?"* he whispered. *"Me?"*

"Yes, you."

"Are you sure?"

"Yes."

"But . . . *why?*"

This time when Judy spoke, Punch heard the same anger in her voice that he had heard so often before. "Da didn't think a girl—me—could do it alone or probably wouldn't even want to. He said you would."

"But, but . . . that's not so!" Punch cried with indignation. "You can. You *have.* Anyway, I don't want even a part of it. It's yours! All of it!"

"No, Punch," Judy said with determination. "Half the show is yours. It was Da's dying wish. And I promised."

"Is *that* why you were so angry at me?"

"Yes."

"Because he gave half to me?"

Judy shook her head. "Because he didn't think enough of me."

"Why . . . why didn't you just tell me?" Punch asked.

"I didn't know how. There I was, sad and mad at Da both. And though I knew it wasn't fair—you didn't know what he'd done—I couldn't help feeling it was your fault, too."

"Da gave half the show . . . to me?" Punch repeated softly, still unable to believe.

"He did, Punch. He did. So do this one last thing. For the show. For yourself. Oh, Punch, truly, it's for yourself."

"But what about *you?*" Punch cried. "Now that you're married and all? What will you do?"

"I don't know," Judy said, and so saying, she left the room.

A few moments later Punch was alone in the barn with Alexander. "Sit down," Punch said as he knelt before the pig. Alexander sat and looked into Punch's face.

"What are we going to do?" Punch asked, his voice pleading. Alexander snuffled. "The sheriff will take me to an orphan's home if I don't do the show," Punch went on. "But if I make him laugh, he'll let me go. But where? I can't stay with Judy. She's gotten married. They won't want me. And, Alexander, I know it's hard to believe, but Da gave half the show to me. Yes, me. He should have given it all to Judy.

"Anyway," Punch whispered, "what could I do with it? I mean, there is no show anymore, is there? The Merry Men have gone. Mrs. McSneed, well . . . And Twig, why, he won't want to have anything to do with it when he learns the show is half mine.

"Sure, there's the old wagon. And some stuff. Belle, too, I suppose, though she's old.

"But, Alexander, here's the worst. If I don't do the show tomorrow, if I don't make Oxnard laugh, he'll take you. Said he'd *eat* you. And oh, Alexander, I think he would!"

Alexander, indifferent, lay down and closed his eyes. Hearing a sound, Punch turned. It was Twig. Partly stooped, ashen-faced, he was standing at the barn door, kneading the brim of his derby as if it were putty.

Punch scrambled to his feet.

"Punch, my darling Punch . . ." Twig began as he advanced, all humble and soft. "Judy's just informed me what Da did. I mean—making you half boss of the show."

Punch was about to protest, but Twig cut him off.

"Hear me out before you speak, lad!" he cried, hysteria edging into his voice. "I wanted you to know that if ever I did you harm, spoke you ill, put you down, why, to be sure, Punch, it wasn't meant for bad. Oh, no! It was all for the love of you, lad, a wanting to strengthen your moral character as any doting dad would do for a much-beloved son.

"It's true, Punch. In all these years my one thought was to give you the decent strength to face a cruel and heartless world."

Twig, moistening his dry lips with the tip of his tongue, crept closer. "Punch," he continued, his voice shaking, his hands trembling, "sweet lad, lad of charity, lad of mercy. Hearken to your most devoted friend. Here's the truth of it. This show is all I have, an old man whose days have not exactly been full of what folks call glory. Oh, sure, back in the old country, I was young and considered gold. And there are folks who'll swear that gold won't tarnish. But I'm here as witness to say it does. It does.

"What do you say, Punch, my darling boy? Will you let me stay with the show? Will you now? Will you be the ever-loving friend to him who thought himself your father?"

Punch was too flabbergasted to answer.

"Tell you what we'll do," Twig went on. "First we'll perform the show for the sheriff. You don't want to go to a foundling home, lad. You wouldn't care for it. Then, with your talent, my experience, as well as Judy's smarts, we'll work to make your future sweet.

"Together, lad, the three of us, we'll do it right. 'Judy, Punch, and Twig,' or 'Punch and Judy.' Or if you'd prefer, just plain 'Punch's Show!' Whatever you want is uncommon fine with me. So say you'll do it, Punch, my boy, for all the love I've cast upon ye!"

Punch, not knowing what else to say, mumbled, "Okay."

"Oh, Punch," Twig cried, "may a bumper basket of blessings settle down upon your godlike head!" And he snatched Punch's hand, covered it with wet kisses, then lurched away.

All Punch could do was stare after him, at his hand, and then at last turn to Alexander. "I'll do it for you," Punch said to the pig. "Just you."

Nine

All during the hot night they practiced, slept a bit, woke, and practiced more. Since there was no time to build a real theater, Twig had Horatio set up the front porch as a stage, the idea being that they could make entrances and exits through the front door. As for the audience—the sheriff—the best chair in the house was set out in the front yard.

Regarding Mrs. McSneed, there was not much choice. Judy decided that since her mother was unaware of what was happening, she'd best remain in her room until the show was over.

By late morning Twig announced that all was ready. He himself had on Doc's old high hat and Blodger's blue tights as well as his own regular plaid coat of many pockets.

"The whole thing is this," the juggler advised. "Don't just think funny and act funny. Keep reminding our audience that we *are* funny. Tell 'em when to laugh, and as the Lord is just and full of mercy, they'll cackle like roosting hens."

And so, shortly after noon—when the sun was at its hottest—Punch saw Sheriff Oxnard arrive. But he was not alone. Five brawny men, all armed, were with him.

Beneath slouch hats, their dirty, unshaven faces presented a menacing cast, as sullen an audience as Punch had ever seen. "He's here," Punch told the others.

They rushed to the window. At the sight of the men Judy gasped. Horatio gulped. Even Twig turned gray.

But just as quickly, the old man rallied. "Not to worry," he cried. "Do as planned, and we're prime. Remember, keep your thinking *funny!*" So saying, he rushed out to meet the audience, going so fast he tripped, almost tumbling down the broken front steps. Recovering, and with the gaping hole of an empty grin fixed upon his face, he cried, "Ah, friends, we're mighty cheered to see you!"

Sheriff Oxnard, refusing to shake Twig's offered hand, nodded curtly. "I brought some pals to see this gag show of yours."

"Most welcome, all!" Twig replied with great exuberance as he surveyed the scowling faces. "I can see you're all more than eager to share the fun and frolic!"

"And the agreement stands," Sheriff Oxnard reminded him. "You people get me to laugh, and that boy with the stupid name goes free. But if I *don't* laugh, then the whole bunch of you—pig included—haul back to New Moosup with me. My friends here will make sure of that."

"Oh, absolutely," Twig replied, trying to ignore the hostile stares of the other men.

"All right, then," the sheriff snapped, "how about some chairs? Or do you expect us to sit in filth?"

"Chairs! Of course!" Twig twittered, and quickly retreated. "Chairs! Chairs!" he called as he barreled into the house. "An audience must have chairs!"

They all scrambled to find unbroken chairs from various parts of the house. Once collected, Twig grabbed

the four of them and hurled himself out the door. This time, however, he caught his foot on a loose board and, taking the chairs with him, plunged forward in a head-long dive. When he landed, he crushed one chair. When he shook his head clear, he found the six men scowling down at him.

"Is that," Sheriff Oxnard demanded, "supposed to be part of your funny stuff?"

"No, sir. Not at all," Twig hastily replied, trying to catch his breath. "Not at all." Hurting all over, but afraid to show it, he picked himself up. Smiling broadly, he dusted off his costume, then clumsily set out the intact chairs. "Two missing," he said sadly.

"Get on with what you've got," the sheriff growled.

"To be sure, sir." Twig backed away, bumping into one of the sheriff's friends who threw him off.

"Begging your pardon, sir," Twig sputtered, and fled into the house.

"It's going to be absolutely fine," Twig said, gasping

for breath. "They're ripe and ready for laughs. Just don't forget: Keep to the script and never stop smiling." That said, he adjusted his costume, gulped down one more breath, and scampered out the door.

For a moment Twig considered his audience. Before him sat the frowning sheriff, thick arms folded over his barrel chest. On both sides sat—two stood—his glowering champions, their belts bristling with guns and ammunition.

"Here's wishing a lovely day to you all!" Twig babbled, tipping his top hat and offering a smile as wide as a yard. "It's a perfect privilege to be greeting so darling a crowd on this sweet day for a dash of merriment and innocent fun. Which reminds me of the feller who meets another feller, and he says, 'How do you do?' And the second feller says, 'To tell the truth, I try to do as little as possible!' Ha-ha!"

No one in the audience so much as blinked.

"Well then," Twig went on, "it's my own particular honor to begin the festivities with a bit of juggle and song, all calculated to bring on the cheerful chuckles."

Tapping his hat to get a rakish angle, Twig, with much mugging, began to sing:

"I took my girl to a fancy ball,
It was a social hop.
We stayed until the folks went out
And the music it did stop.
Then to a restaurant we went,
The best one on the street,
And though she said she wasn't hungry,
This is what she et:

Twelve oysters raw, a plate of slaw,
A chicken and a roast,
Some asparagus with apple sass,

And soft-shell crabs on toast,
A big box stew with chickens, too;
Her hunger was that immense.
And when she called for pie, I thought I'd die—

For I had but fifty cents!"

Now Twig plucked some ears of corn from his coat
pockets and started to juggle while he sang the second
verse.

"When I asked her what she'd have to drink,
She smiled at me her thanks,
And though she pleaded she wasn't thirsty,
Here's exactly what she drank:

A glass of gin, a whisky skin,
Some ginger pop with rum on top,
Plus a schooner full of beer,
A glass of ale, and a gin cocktail.
Oh, she ought to have had some sense,
For when she called for more,
I near dropped to the floor—

For I had but fifty cents!"

Twig added some shuffling dance steps to the juggling, while he went on:

"I told her that my head did ache
And I did not care to eat,
Expecting every moment to get kicked upon the
*   street.*
Then she said next time she'd bring her folks,

So we could really have some fun!
But when I gave the clerk my fifty cents,
This is what he done:

He smashed my nose and tore my clothes,
He hit me on the jaw,
And put my eyes in mourning deep,
And swept me with the floor.
He grabbed me where my pants were loose
and kicked me o'er the fence.
So take my advice, don't eat out twice—

When you have but fifty cents!''

Sweating profusely, laughing loudly, Twig pranced up and down, repeating the last two lines:

"So take my advice, don't eat out twice
When you have but fifty cents!''

With a final click of his heels and a tossing away of corncobs, Twig bowed low, grinning as widely as his mouth could stretch. And though his audience offered up not so much as one smile, he hopped back from the porch into the house.

Next was Horatio's turn. Clothed in sailor's garb, wearing a green wig, he poked his head around the door and gazed bleakly out at the frowning men. He pulled back hastily. "Judy," he said, his voice rattled with nervousness, "I don't think I can do it."

Punch was sitting on the parlor floor putting Alexander into a nightgown. Horatio's fright filled him with alarm.

"Of course, you can do it!" Twig interceded. "Those

are simple tricks I've taught you. You can't miss. Besides, you have to loosen them up for what follows. Remember, just stay with what I told you to do, and above all, boyo, *keep being funny.*"

Horatio pleaded silently to Judy. "It's only this once," she said kindly.

Since there was no avoiding it, Horatio stepped timidly onto the porch, moving gingerly around the loose boards. When he reached the front steps, he lifted his eyes to his audience, trying to avoid the stern gaze of the sheriff, who was sitting right before him. With fumbling hands, he rummaged in his pockets and pulled out a pack of grimy playing cards.

Before he could do anything, the sheriff yelled, "Horatio Cuthwhip, you ought to be ashamed of yourself! Married, you say! To a circus girl! Your father will like hearing that, won't he? Want my advice, boy? Run off while you can!"

Horatio, trying to ignore the taunts, cleared his throat, and with shaking hands held up the deck of playing cards. "I have here," he began, "a deck of cards—"

"Playing cards!" the sheriff roared. "So you're gambling, too, are you?"

"Here is a card," Horatio persisted, "which I'll hold up . . ." But with his fingers shaking so, the entire deck spurted out of his hands like a geyser of water. Desperately, he tried to gather up the cards, holding some in his mouth, others under his arms, only to drop them all over again.

At this the sheriff heaved himself up and marched to the porch. "Give me those things!" he demanded. Horatio attempted to retreat. Oxnard was too quick. He snatched the few remaining cards from Horatio's hands, tore them into confetti, and flung the bits away. Then he turned and marched back to his seat.

Horatio, unable to move, his mouth agape with shock, stammered, "But . . . but . . . you were supposed to pick just . . . *one.*" At that he fled back into the house, where Judy tried to console him.

It was Punch's turn next.

"Punch, my lad," Twig announced, "it's time for your famous dance." Punch was wearing Doc's dinner jacket and trousers—both too large—as well as Zun's plumed helmet. Twig had to turn him toward the door, open it, and push him onto the porch.

Full of fear, floating on a sea of nausea, Punch crept to the porch edge. He tried to look at the audience, but the frightful faces before him caused his every muscle to cramp. "A dance," he croaked, but stood still.

"Get on with it, boy," Oxnard growled. "It's a long way to New Moosup."

Startled into motion, Punch jumped back, only to plunge one foot through a rotten porch board. Frantic, he tried to pull out the leg, but found it jammed against the jagged edge of another board, which bit into his calf. Gripping his leg with both hands, he yanked. The board ripped up, leaving a gaping hole. As for his foot, it came free, but it hurt badly.

"Smile!" Punch heard Twig hiss from behind the door. *"Be funny!"*

Punch, even as he tried to keep from putting his full weight down on his throbbing foot, inched back toward the front of the porch and forced himself to grin.

"Are you going to dance or not?" the sheriff barked.

"Yes, sir . . . I am," Punch mumbled, and flung his arms wide to either side. In so doing, he struck his right hand against the nearest porch column. It smarted terribly. Instinctively, he sought to suck away the sting. As he did, he forgot about his foot and pressed down full-weight. That made his leg buckle. Down the steps he tumbled, head over heels, the top hat ramming over his ears so as to completely blind him. By the time he stopped moving, he was groggy, his head was spinning, he could see nothing. In a panic, he grasped the brim of his hat and attempted to lift it from his eyes. The brim tore off. Exhausted, it was all he could do to breathe.

"Maybe *you* think that's funny," Oxnard sneered— Punch was sprawled two feet from him—"but I say it's an affront to decent folks. Get up and do what you're supposed to do before I call this whole wretched business off. Twiger!" he roared. "Get this mistake out of here!"

Twig, bowing and scraping, hurried out of the house. "Not to worry," he called. "Accidents happen!"

Grasping Punch—for the boy was helpless—Twig attempted to yank him up, only to stagger under the weight and fall, too.

Now it was Horatio, urged by Judy, who scrambled out to help. But as Horatio rushed forward, he caught one of his own feet in the hole Punch had made, which caused *him* to shoot forward with such speed that he did a complete flip and landed faceup in front of the sheriff and his friends. There he lay, thoroughly stunned.

Sheriff Oxnard jumped to his feet. His friends did the same. "Come on, then! We haven't laughed. You're all under arrest!"

"No, no!" Twig wailed. "We're not done, and the best is yet to come. I promise!"

Reluctantly, the sheriff sat down. So did the others.

Somehow, Twig managed to get Punch up and into the house. Judy did the same for Horatio.

Punch sat slumped over, while Twig danced about. "The man's all primed up, boy," the old juggler insisted. "He's just restraining himself. He *wants* to laugh. He *needs* to laugh. One more touch, and you'll send him over hilarity hill!"

Groggy, Punch shook his head.

"It's the truth, lad!" Twig cried. "You're a delicious dunce! A fool for all fancies! A buffoon that shines bright only once in a million moons!"

"No more," Punch begged with a shake of his head. "No more."

"You can't give up, lad," Twig screamed at him. "Your life won't be worth the living in the place he'll lodge you. You'll perish! You'll die! You'll spend your eternity doing dances for the devil!"

"I don't care!"

At that the old man grabbed Punch by his shirt and shook him hard. "Boyo," he said in a rage, "I made the bargain with him in good faith! It's not just you he'll take. Don't you understand, it's me, too!" In wild frustration, he flung Punch away.

"Judy," he screamed. "We're running out of time! *Do something!*"

At that moment the door to the inner room burst open. Mrs. McSneed appeared. "The Queen of Tipperary cannot sleep!" she announced.

Judy covered her face with her hands.

"I'll take care of her," Twig cried. "Just make Punch go back." Off he went with Mrs. McSneed, shouting, "Be quiet now, O lovely queen!" as he led the woman back into her room.

Judy kneeled before Punch. "Punch," she said. "You mustn't stop now."

"I want to die," Punch whispered. There was not a part of him, inside or out, that was not hurting.

"Punch," Judy said, shaking him gently, "you are like a brother to me now, aren't you?"

Punch was not sure he'd heard right. "A *what?*" he said.

"A brother . . ."

"I'm nobody's brother," Punch said. "Nobody's!"

"Believe me, Punch, you're mine." Punch stared at her. "You have to save yourself," Judy went on. "And us, too! Please, Punch, *please.* I do love you so. Save yourself!"

Just then the front door was yanked open by the sheriff. "You finishing your act or not?" he demanded.

"One moment!" Judy yelled.

The sheriff retreated.

"Do you . . . really love me?" Punch stammered to Judy.

"Oh, yes, Punch, yes!"

"As a brother?"

At that Judy flung her arms about Punch and burst into tears.

141

As Punch felt her arms about him, as he heard her words, "Oh, yes, Punch, yes!" and felt her hot tears on his face, the only thing he experienced was a bolt of happiness such as he had never felt before. Right then and right there Punch knew love, felt love, believed love. It gave him such a sense of light and joy, such giddiness, that it set the very tips of his fingers to tingling.

Then, as though through a fog, Punch heard Twig shout, "For the blessed Lord's sake, boyo, will you bestir yourself!"

Smiling, *laughing,* Punch jumped to his feet. *"Yes!"* he cried. *"Yes!"*

Ten

It was a light-headed, cocky Punch who stepped upon
the porch again. Over his hair, pulled tight, he had a
white stocking to suggest baldness. A red ball was tied
to his nose with string. His lips were smudged with
purple rouge, while black rings had been drawn with
charcoal around his eyes. On his feet were slippers much
too long. A pillow had been stuffed under his crimson
jacket to make him look fat. His legs bore white bloomers. In his right hand he held a string tied to Alexander.
The pig wore a nightgown as well as a baby bonnet
around his head. And in his left hand Punch carried the
slap-stick.

Now when Punch came out of the door, he was so
excited he truly pranced, kicked his heels, and spun
about even as he took care to avoid the porch holes and
rotten wood. He even laughed. It was real laughter, too.

Catching his breath, he bellowed, ''Hello! How do
you do. My name is Mr. Punch,'' and he threw back
his head and laughed.

The sheriff sat up. ''Get on with it,'' he snarled.

Punch grinned broadly. ''Here is Judy's baby,'' he
said, and looked down at Alexander. Alexander snuffled
the air.

"I must admit," Punch continued, "she's a handsome baby. Indeed, she looks just like Judy. Oh, lovely baby! Beautiful baby!

"But you see," Punch went on, "I hate Judy. Judy is my wife and oh, how I hate her more than anyone in the whole world. She's the meanest one in the world. The stupidest and the ugliest!

"Judy was so mean and so cruel to me that I stole her baby. Of course, I made sure Judy knows I stole her baby so that when she comes after me I'll be ready for her!" Punch held up the slap-stick and rattled it.

"Believe me," he continued, "I'll use this stick to make sure that Judy gets all that she deserves. Will it hurt her? I hope so. Oh, I hope so!" And again Punch laughed, real laughter—he was having that much fun!

To demonstrate what the slap-stick would do, Punch swung it hard against one of the columns. The result was a tremendous crack. He laughed again.

"Come on," the sheriff called as he shifted restlessly in his seat, "get to the funny part!"

"Very well," Punch said, "I'll leave Baby here. Judy will come soon enough." Saying, "Stay!" to Alexander, he stepped behind one of the columns. "Don't tell Judy I'm here," he said to the audience.

"Judy!" Punch brayed. "Ju-dy! Someone has found your baby. Yoo-hoooo, wifey! Come find your pretty baby!"

Judy stepped onto the porch. Her red hair was braided and tied with golden ribbons. She was wearing a baggy, blue gingham dress and oversized boots. A large false nose was tied around her head.

She began to wander about the porch, crying, "Oh, Baby! Who has seen my beautiful baby! That rascal husband of mine, Mr. Punch, has stolen my baby. Oh,

144

how I hate Mr. Punch. He's the meanest person in the world. And the ugliest. And the stupidest! If ever I catch him, I'll beat him to a pulp!''

Suddenly Judy spied Alexander. ''There is my beautiful baby! There she is!'' With her back to where he was hiding, Judy bent over and hugged Alexander. Alexander grunted.

Now, when Judy bent over, Punch stepped from behind the column and whacked her behind with the slapstick. It made its regular big sound. Then he jumped behind the column.

Judy stood up. ''A flea!'' she said. ''A flea has bitten me! But never mind; it's my baby I care about.''

Once again Judy bent over and hugged the pig. And once again Punch stepped out from his hiding place and whacked her behind—then jumped around the post.

Judy leaped up. ''Was that another flea?'' she asked. Then she bent over to hug Alexander. But this time when she bent over, she looked back through her legs. Even as she did, Punch stepped out as if to hit her.

''Ah-ha!'' Judy cried, looking up at Punch from between her legs. ''It's you, you rascal!''

Even as Punch was about to strike her, Judy jumped around so they were face to face, fake nose to fake nose.

''What's that in your hand?'' she demanded.

''A magic wand,'' Punch replied, waving the slapstick.

''What kind of magic does it do?''

''It turns everything inside out.''

''What does that mean?''

''If you hit someone with it, it will make her beautiful.''

''Beautiful, you say?''

''And happy. And full of love!''

"May I see it?"

"Do you want to see it on your backside or on your head?"

"My hand."

"Very well, hold out your hand." Judy did so. Punch whacked it.

"Ouch! Ouch! Ouch!" Judy cried.

Punch grimaced with pleasure. "There," he said, "don't you feel better already?"

Judy looked to the audience. "This rascal has tricked me, but now I shall trick him. I'll grab that stick and use it on *him!*" To Punch she said, "What a clever magic wand. Do it again." Once more she held out her hand.

Punch, as bidden, brought down the stick, but slowly. And that time—just as they had rehearsed—Judy grabbed the slap-stick and yanked it away. Pretending to be startled, Punch jumped back.

"Now," Judy cried, brandishing the slap-stick, "I'll make *you* beautiful! And happy! And full of love for me!'' Drawing the stick back, she prepared to strike. But as she did, she struck the stick against the post right behind her. When she did, the small block of wood that held the two sticks apart dropped out.

Judy did not see it fall. But Punch did, and since he knew what *that* meant, he froze in terror. Judy, however, not knowing what had happened, continued to follow Twig's script. With a mighty crack she brought the slapstick down hard across Punch's head.

The blow sent Punch reeling. He was just about to cry out—the pain was that awful—when he caught a glimpse of the sheriff's frowning face. And he remembered Twig's advice. *''Funny!''* Punch bellowed. ''That's very funny!''

Wasting no time, Judy quickly followed up her first blow with a second. ''I'm glad you think so, Mr. Punch, because here's a blow to make you beau-ti-ful!'' With that she whacked Punch over the head again.

Punch staggered back, saying, ''Oh, that's so funny! You don't know how happy it makes me! Do it again!''

''Then this,'' cried Judy, leaping forward and giving Punch another blow, ''will make you even happier!''

Tormented with pain, unable to take another blow, Punch tried to get away. But with his face running with tears of charcoal blacking that made him unable to see where he was going, he slammed blindly into a column. Back he bounced, only to plunge a foot down through a rotten floorboard. And there he stuck.

At that Judy pounced forward and began to flail Punch with all her might. ''Here's a kiss and a hug!'' she cried with two tremendous whacks.

''Ha-ha!'' Punch laughed as he cowered beneath the blows. Off went his nose. Off went his head stocking.

''And here,'' Judy cried, ''is a final kiss so you know

just how much I love you!'' With that she gave Punch the greatest blow of all.

''This,'' Punch screamed in terror, ''this is the funniest thing in the whole world!''

It was then that Sheriff Oxnard, spewing spit from behind tightly pressed lips, exploded into laughter. And once his laughter came, it could not be stopped. It thundered. It roared. His feet pounded up and down. His eyes squeezed shut. His arms dropped helplessly by his sides.

And when the sheriff began to laugh, his friends began to laugh—screaming, raucous laughter. Contagious laughter it was, laughter that doubled—tripled—them over. They laughed until they choked—which made them laugh again. So catching was the laughter that when they looked at one another, it made them laugh again and more. Their sides ached. Their chests heaved. Their heads spun. Two fell off their chairs. That redoubled their laughs. One laughed so hard he kicked up his feet, tumbled backward, and almost broke his neck. It only made them laugh again.

As the laughter poured out, flooded out, Judy in raptures of joy and triumph, whacked and whacked away at Punch. And Punch, knowing that Judy's painful blows were the cause of the sheriff's laughter and that this laughter meant liberation, that the more she struck him, the more free he was, why, he laughed with joy even as he cried with pain until, unable to endure one drop more, he screamed with all his soul, ''Judy! Stop! Please! *You're really killing me!*''

And *that* remark brought the sheriff and all his men to their greatest peak of laughter yet.

So great was the uproar that Twig, unable to restrain

his joy and relief, ran out onto the porch and joined in with *his* laughter.

Then Horatio came out, and when he saw everybody laughing, he, too, began to laugh.

Even Alexander began to grunt and squeal.

It was at that moment that Mrs. McSneed staggered out the door. The look upon her face was one of great bewilderment. Her hair hung loose. Her shift was rent.

"Laughter!" she cried, lifting her arms toward heaven. "My king has returned!"

Her piercing voice brought all to a halt. Judy stopped beating Punch. Horatio froze. Twig dared not breathe. Even the sheriff and his men paused to stare at the strange figure who stood before them.

Mrs. McSneed stumbled forward. "Where is he?" she demanded. "Who is the laughing one?" Lunging forward, she bumped into Punch, which caused her to go wheeling about and crash into a column. It was the same column Punch had weakened. This time, however, the column dropped off its footing. With that, the entire porch—roof, floor, columns, everything—collapsed.

Sheriff Oxnard and his men rushed to pull away the wreckage. First to be freed was Horatio. Then he joined in and helped release Judy and Alexander. Working frantically, they untangled Twig and Punch. Last to be uncovered was Mrs. McSneed.

When at last they turned her over, she opened her eyes and looked up at Judy. "Judy, my dear," she said, "I know poor Da died. But has anything happened since?"

Eleven

Two weeks later Belle stood between the wagon shafts as Mrs. McSneed gently stroked her mane. Twig, derby pushed to the back of his head, was by her side. Horatio, meanwhile, finished loading the last of the equipment into the wagon.

As for Judy and Punch, they were off a bit by themselves. Punch was looking down at the ground where Alexander lay sprawled asleep.

Judy studied Punch awhile longer, then she said, "I promise I'll be okay."

Punch lifted a shoulder. "I hope so," he said.

"Punch," she said, "the old show *is* gone. Like Da. In this show it's you who'll make it work. You know you're good, don't you?" She gave him a little shake.

Shyly, without quite facing her, he looked up. "I guess," he said.

She chucked him under the chin. "More," she insisted. "They loved you in Farktwist, didn't they? Wouldn't let you stop."

That time Punch smiled. "I know," he said.

"And you'll have Mama and Twig, too."

"And Alexander," Punch reminded her. Then he added, "But it would be better with you."

"Look at me," Judy whispered.

Punch faced her.

"For my whole life," she said, "I've traveled with the show. Da's show. I'm not sure what else there is for me. So I need to try staying put. For a bit anyway. Maybe I'll like it. Maybe I won't. And while you're keeping the show together, Horatio and I will be here. When winter comes, you'll all come back. Here. To home. Then, we'll all decide what to do. Okay?"

"Okay."

"Punch," Judy said with a smile, "even a fool needs a home."

"I know."

"And Punch," Judy went on, "I do love you like my true brother. You know that, too, don't you?"

"Yes."

"And you promise to love me always as a sister, won't you?"

"Yes."

"Then that's the way it will be," she said. "Punch *and* Judy."

"Punch *with* Judy," Punch returned.

At that they hugged each other.

"Punch!" Mrs. McSneed cried. "Come on now. We have to be leaving, and I'm not going anywhere without your laughter!"

Gently, Judy pushed Punch away.

Suddenly, Punch reached into his pocket and pulled out the dollar coin. He offered it to Judy.

"What's that?" she asked.

"It's . . . my good-luck charm," he said. "I want you to keep it for me."

When she took it, Punch turned, squared his shoulders, and cried, "All right! Let's go!"

The wagon started to roll. Punch reached over and gently tweaked one of Alexander's ears. With a snort, the pig woke, shook his great head, then scrambled to his feet.

With Alexander trotting at his side, Punch hurried after the wagon. He dared not look back. Instead, he looked up at the wagon side. It had been repainted:

Mr. PUNCH AND HIS SHOW
WITH Mr. TWIGLET,
RENOWNED SINGER AND JUGGLER
AND
Mrs. McSNEED!
CONTORTIONIST SUPREME
WHO IS ACTUALLY
THE KING OF TIPPERARY'S WIDOW

ALSO STARRING
ALEXANDER–the WONDER PIG
AND BEST OF ALL
PUNCH
WORLD'S GREATEST FOOL
* * *
GUARANTEED TO MAKE YOU LAUGH!!!

AVI, known for the imaginative range of his work, has recently published *Beyond the Western Sea, Book One: The Escape From Home,* the first part of a three-part serial novel. Two of Avi's many other novels include the Newbery Honor Books *The True Confessions of Charlotte Doyle* and *Nothing But the Truth.*

Avi currently lives in Denver, Colorado.